Mayne Reid

The Death Shot

Vol. 1

Mayne Reid

The Death Shot
Vol. 1

ISBN/EAN: 9783337346911

Printed in Europe, USA, Canada, Australia, Japan

Cover: Foto ©Andreas Hilbeck / pixelio.de

More available books at **www.hansebooks.com**

THE DEATH SHOT.

A Romance of Forest and Prairie.

BY

CAPTAIN MAYNE REID,

AUTHOR OF "THE HEADLESS HORSEMAN."

IN THREE VOLUMES.
VOL. I.

LONDON:
CHAPMAN AND HALL, 193, PICCADILLY.
1873.

CONTENTS OF VOL. I.

CHAPTER   PAGE

PROLOGUE 1

I. TWO SORTS OF SLAVE-OWNERS . . . 8

II. TWO GOOD GIRLS 19

III. A FOREST POST-BOX 26

IV. A PHOTOGRAPH IN THE FOREST . . . 35

V. UNDER THE CYPRESS 46

VI. A COON-CHASE INTERRUPTED . . . 55

VII. THE ASSASSIN IN RETREAT . . . 65

VIII. THE COON-HUNTER AT HOME . . . 72

IX. UNDER THE MAGNOLIA 81

X. THE WRONG MAN 92

XI. "WHY COMES HE NOT?" 100

XII. A LAST LOOK AT LOVED SCENES . . 110

XIII. WHAT HAS BECOME OF THE CORPSE? . 116

XIV. THE SLEEP OF THE ASSASSIN . . . 131

XV. THE HOUSE OF MOURNING . . . 138

XVI. A SOUTH-WESTERN SHERIFF . . . 145

XVII. THE "BELLE OF NATCHEZ" . . . 152

XVIII. SEIZED BY SPECTRAL ARMS . . 164

CHAPTER		PAGE
XIX.	WHAT BECAME OF HER	171
XX.	A BACKWOODS JURY IN DELIBERATION .	181
XXI.	THE COON-HUNTER CONSCIENCE-STRICKEN .	190
XXII.	A VOLUNTARY WITNESS . . .	197
XXIII.	CONVINCING EVIDENCE . . .	203
XXIV.	TO THE GAOL	214
XXV.	A CHOICE OF SONS-IN-LAW	222
XXVI.	NEWS FROM NATCHEZ	231
XXVII.	SPECTRES IN THE STREET	241
XXVIII.	THE "CHOCTAW CHIEF" . . .	256
XXIX.	THE MURDERER UNMASKED . .	271
XXX.	"WILL YOU BE ONE OF US?" . .	282

THE DEATH SHOT.

PROLOGUE.

A PRAIRIE, treeless, shrubless, smooth as a sleeping sea. Grass upon it; but so short, that the smallest quadruped might not cross over without being seen. Even a crawling reptile could scarce find concealment among its tufts.

Objects are upon it—sufficiently visible to be distinguished at some distance. But they are of a character scarce deserving a glance from the passing traveller. He would hardly deem it worth while to turn his eyes toward a pack of prairie wolves—*coyotes*—much less go in chase of them.

With vultures soaring above, he might be more

disposed to hesitate and reflect. The foul birds and filthy beasts, seen together, would be proof of prey—that some quarry had fallen upon the plain. It might be a stricken stag, a prong-horn antelope, or a wild horse crippled by some mischance due to his headlong nature.

Believing it any of these, the traveller would give loose rein to his steed and ride onward; leaving the beasts and birds to their banquet.

There is no traveller passing over the prairie in question; no human being in sight. But there are wolves grouped upon the ground, and vultures hovering in the air above them.

And not unseen by human eye. For there is one sees—one who has reason to fear them.

Their eager, excited movements show that they are anticipating a repast; at the same time their attitudes tell, they have not yet commenced it.

Something appears in their midst. At intervals they approach it: the birds swoopingly from above, the beasts crouchingly along the sward. They go close, almost to touching it;

then suddenly withdraw, starting back as in affright!

After a time they return again, but only to be frayed as before. And so on, in a series of approaches and recessions.

What can be the object thus keeping them off? Surely no common quarry, as the dead body of deer, antelope, or mustang? It cannot be this; nor yet carcass of any kind. It cannot be a thing that is dead. Nor does it look like anything alive. Seen from a distance it resembles a human head; nearer, the resemblance grows stronger; close up, it is complete. Certainly, it *is* a human head—*the head of a man!*

What is there in this to cause surprise? A man's head seen upon a Texan prairie! Nothing, if lying there scalpless. It would only prove that some ill-starred individual—traveller, trapper, or hunter of wild horses—has been struck down by the savages; and afterwards decapitated, as well as scalped.

But this head—if head it be—is *not* scalped. It still carries its hair—a fine chevelure, waving and profuse. Nor is it lying along the ground, as it naturally would, abandoned, after being despoiled of its trophy. On the contrary, it stands erect upon the sward—the chin almost touching the surface—square, as if still upon the shoulders from which it has been separated! With cheeks pallid or blood-bedaubed, and eyes closed or glassy, this—the position—need not so much surprise. But there is neither pallor, nor blood-stain on the cheeks; and the eyes are not closed, not glassed. They are glancing — glaring — rolling. *By Heavens! the head is alive!*

No wonder the wolves start back in affright; no wonder the vultures, after swooping down, ply their wings in quick nervous stroke, and soar up again! The strange thing seems to puzzle both —baffles their instinct, and keeps them at bay.

Still know they, or seem to fancy, 'tis flesh and blood. Sight and scent tell them it is; by both they cannot be deceived.

And living flesh it must be? A death's head could neither flash its eyes, nor cause them to turn in their sockets. Besides, the predatory creatures have other evidence of its being alive. At intervals there is opened a mouth, showing two rows of white teeth. From between comes a shout that startles, and sends them afar.

The cry is only put forth, when they approach too threateningly near—evidently intended to keep them at a distance. It has done so for most part of a day.

Twilight approaching, spreads its purple tints over the prairie. It is on. There is no change in the attitude of the assailed, or assailants. There is light enough to show the flash of those fiery eyes; whose glance of menace still masters the voracious instincts of the animals.

Strange spectacle! The head of a man, without any body—set square upon the ground; with eyes in it that scintillate and see, a mouth that opens, and shows teeth; a throat from which issue sounds evidently of human intonation: around this object of almost supernatural aspect, a group of grey wolves, and over it a flock of black vultures!

Through the day, and into twilight, the tableau

remains unchanged. Only a change in the disposition of the figures—in the attitudes of the beasts and birds. The head keeps its place and position. It makes no motion, save the parting of the lips, and the rolling of the eyeballs.

On a Texan prairie twilight is short. There are no mountains or high hills intervening—no obliquity in the sun's diurnal course, to lengthen out the day. When the golden orb sinks behind the horizon, a short-lived light of purplish tint succeeds—then night.

Night approaches. It is on.

With the darkness comes a change. The vultures, obedient to their customary habit—not nocturnal—take departure from the spot, and wing their way to some well-known roosting-place. On the contrary, the wolves stay. Night is the time best suited to their ravening instincts. Under its shadows they may have more hope of at length devouring that thing of spherical shape, that by shouts and scowling glances has so long held them aloof.

To their discomfiture, the twilight is very

soon succeeded by a magnificent moon; whose silvery effulgence shed over the prairie almost equals the light of day. It shows the eyes yet angrily glancing; while in the nocturnal stillness that cry, sent through the parted lips, is as awe-inspiring as ever.

It still keeps the assailants at bay.

And, now, more than ever does the tableau appear strange—more than ever unlike reality. Under the moonlight, with a filmy haze spread over the prairie sward, the human head seems magnified to the dimensions of the Sphinx; while, from the same cause, the coyotés look as large as Canadian stags!

In truth, a singular spectacle—one full of weird mystery!

Who can explain it?

CHAPTER I.

TWO SORTS OF SLAVE-OWNERS.

In the old slave-owning times of the Southern United States—happily now no more—there was much grievance to humanity; proud oppression upon the one side, and sad suffering on the other.

It is true, that the majority of the slave proprietors were humane men. Some of them even philanthropic, in their way, and inclined towards giving to the unholy institution a colour of *patriarchism*. The idea—delusive, as intended to delude—is old as slavery itself; at the same time, modern as Mormonism; where it has had its latest, and coarsest illustration.

Though it cannot be denied, that the slavery of the States was in many instances of a mild type, neither can it be questioned, that there were cases of lamentable harshness—even to inhumanity. There were slave-owners who were kind, and slave-owners who were cruel.

Not far from the town of Natchez, in the State of Mississippi, lived two planters; whose lives illustrated the extremes of these two types. Though their estates lay adjacent, their characters were as opposite as could well be conceived in the scale of manhood and morality. Colonel Archibald Armstrong—a true Southerner of the old Virginian aristocracy, who had entered Mississippi State when the Choctaw Indians evacuated it—was a model of the kind slave-master; while Ephraim Darke—a Massachusetts man, who had moved thither at a much later period—was a fair specimen of the cruel. Coming from the New England States, sprung from the Puritans—a people whose descendants have made both profession and sacrifice in the cause of negro emancipation—this may seem strange. It is, however, a common tale; which no traveller through the Southern States can help hearing.

Every day will he be told, that the hardest task-master of the slave is either one who has been a slave himself, or a descendant of the Pilgrim Fathers, who landed on Plymouth Rock! Having a respect for many points in the character of these same Pilgrim Fathers, I would fain think the accusation untrue, and that Ephraim Darke was an exception.

In his case, there was no falsehood in it—none whatever. Throughout the Mississippi valley, there was nothing more vile than his treatment of the black bondsmen, whose hard lot it was to have him for their master. Around his courts, and in his cotton-fields, the crack of the whip was heard almost continually—its thong sharply felt by the sable-skinned victims of his caprice or malice. The "cow-hide" was constantly carried by himself, his son, and overseer. None of the three ever went abroad without that pliant, painted switch—a very emblem of devilish cruelty—in their hands; never came home without having used it in the castigation of some unfortunate "darkey," whose evil star had thrown him in their track, while making the rounds of the plantation.

It was the very reverse with his neighbour, Archibald Armstrong—whose slaves seldom went to bed without a prayer upon their lips, that said, "God bress de good massa;" while the poor whipped bondmen of Ephraim Darke, their backs still smarting from the lash, nightly lay down, not always to sleep, but always with curses on their lips.

Alas! the old story, of like cause bringing about like result, is what must be chronicled in this case. The man of the Devil prospered; while he of God decayed. Colonel Armstrong, open-hearted, generous, indulging in a profuse hospitality, lived outside the income accruing from the culture of his cotton-fields. In time he became the debtor of Ephraim Darke, who lived within his.

There was not much intimacy or friendship between the two men. The proud Virginian, come of an old Highland family—gentry in the colonial times—felt some contempt for his neighbour, a descendant of the Mayflower steerage passengers.

For all this, he was not above accepting a loan from Darke, which the latter had been eager to give. The Massachusetts man had long coveted the Southerner's fine estate; and knew that a mortgage-deed is the first entering of a wedge, in time pretty sure to bring about possession of the *fee simple.*

So stood things between these two neighbouring planters. Darke had determined on becoming the proprietor of both plantations; while the affairs of Armstrong, gradually growing desperate, had at length reached a point that promised his neighbour all he had been scheming to obtain. The debtor had fallen behind in the payment of interest. The mortgage could at any moment be foreclosed. Colonel Armstrong was in danger of losing his estate.

At this crisis came a circumstance, likely to modify, if not altogether defeat, the design of the creditor. Ephraim Darke had a son approaching manhood, by name Richard, by nature like himself, only of a still inferior type of humanity. For the grasping selfishness of the extreme Puritan is not improved by mixture with the opposite extreme of Southern licentiousness; and in the character of Richard Darke the two were commingled. Mean in the matter of personal expenditure, he was at the same time of dissipated and disorderly habits; the associate of the poker-playing and cock-fighting fraternity of the neighbourhood; one of its wildest youth, without any of those generous traits sometimes coupled with such a character.

He was Ephraim Darke's only son—therefore heir-presumptive to all his property—slaves and plantation. Being thoroughly in his father's confidence, he was aware of the probability of a proximate reversion to the slaves and plantation of Colonel Armstrong.

But, much as Richard Darke liked money, there was something he coveted more. This was Colonel Armstrong's daughter. There were two of them, Helen and Jessie, both pretty girls. Helen, the elder, was more than pretty, she was beautiful—by all acknowledged as the beauty of the neighbourhood.

Richard Darke was in love with her, as much as his selfish heart would allow—perhaps the only unselfish passion he had ever felt. His father sanctioned, or at all events did not oppose it. For this wild, wicked youth had gained a wonderful ascendancy over a parent, who had trained him to trickery equalling his own.

With the power of creditor over debtor—a debt that could be demanded at any moment—a mortgage to the full amount and not easily transferred—the Darkes seemed to have the vantage-ground, and might dictate their own terms.

The son had been for some time paying his attentions to Helen Armstrong, whenever an opportunity occurred—at balls, *barbecues*, and the like; of late, also, at her father's house. There, the power spoken of gave him admittance; while the consciousness of possessing it, hindered him from noticing the reluctance with which he was received. For all, he could not fail to per-

ceive, that his assiduities were coldly met by her
to whom his homage was extended.

He wondered why, too. He knew that Helen
Armstrong had many admirers. It could not be
otherwise with one so beautiful, and, beside, so
gifted. But among them there was none for
whom she had shown the slightest partiality.
This was notorious. Darke himself had conceived a suspicion, that a young man, named
Clancy—son of a decayed Irish gentleman, living
near—had found favour in her eyes. Still, it
was but a suspicion; and Clancy had gone to
Texas the year before—sent, it was said, by his
father, to look out for a new home. The latter
had since died, leaving his widow sole occupant
of an humble tenement, with a small holding of
land near the borders of the Armstrong estate.

There was a report that young Clancy was soon
coming back—was, indeed, every day expected.
But what could it matter ? The proud planter,
Armstrong, was not the man to bestow his
daughter upon a "poor white" — as Richard
Darke scornfully styled his suspected rival.

Feeling confident of this, as also in the vantage-ground he himself held, the suitor of Helen
Armstrong had resolved upon bringing things to
an issue. His love for her had become a passion,
the stronger for being checked. Her coldness
might be but coquetry. He hoped and fancied it
was; for he had no lack of either self-esteem or
assurance. And he had reason for both. He
was immensely rich, or would be when his father
died. He was not ill-looking, but rather the reverse; and he had made more than one conquest
among the young ladies of the neighbourhood.
It might be, Miss Armstrong's haughty disposition hindered her from being demonstrative?
Perhaps she loved him without giving sign?

For months he had been cogitating in this un-
certain way, and had at length determined to
bring matters to a crisis.

One morning he mounted his horse; rode across
the boundary-line between the two plantations,
and on to Colonel Armstrong's house; requested
an interview with the colonel's eldest daughter;
obtained it; made a declaration of his love; asked

her to have him for a husband : and received for
response a chilling negative.

As he went back through the woods, the birds
were trilling among the trees. It was their merry
morning lay, but it gave him no gladness. There
was still ringing in his ears that harsh monosyllable " *no.*" The wild-wood songsters seemed to
echo it, as if mockingly; the blue jay and red car-
dinal scolding him for intrusion on their domain.

After crossing the boundary between the two
plantations, he reined up his horse, and looked
back. His brow was black with chagrin; his
lips white with rage. It was suppressed no
longer. Curses came hissing through his teeth,
along with the words—

"In less than six weeks these woods will be
mine; and d—— me if I don't shoot every bird
that roosts in them! Then, Miss Helen Armstrong, you'll not be so conceited of yourself. It
will be different, when you havn't got a roof
over your head ! So good-bye, sweetheart; good-
bye to you !"

"Now, dad !" he continued, in fancy apostrophising his father, "now you can take your own way, as you've been long wanting. Yes, my respected parent; you are free to put in the execution—the sheriff's officers—anything you like."

Angrily grinding his teeth, he dug the spurs into his horse's ribs, and rode on—the short, bitter syllable still ringing in his ears.

CHAPTER II.

TWO GOOD GIRLS.

RICHARD DARKE had not long parted from the presence of the lady who so laconically rejected him, when another stood by her side.

A man also, though no rival to him,—neither lover nor suitor. The venerable white-haired gentleman, who came into the room, was Helen Armstrong's father.

His voice, on entering, told that he had a suspicion of what had been Darke's errand.

He was soon made certain by his daughter freely confessing it.

He said in reply:—

"I supposed that to be the fellow's purpose; though, at such an early hour, I might have feared its being worse."

2—2

" Worse !   Feared !   Father, what could you have feared ?"

" Never mind, Helen ; nothing that concerns you.   Tell me : in what way did you give him the answer ?"

" In one little word.   I simply said *no.*"

" That little word will be enough.   Oh Heaven! what will become of us ?"

" Father !" exclaimed the beautiful girl, laying her hand upon his shoulder, with a searching look into his eyes; " why do you speak thus ? Are you angry with me for refusing him? Surely you would not wish me to be the wife of Richard Darke ?"

" You do not love him, Helen ?"

" Love him !   Can you ask ?   Who could love that man ?"

" Then you would not marry him ?"

" Would not—I could not.   He has no heart but the heart of a villain.   I would prefer death to such a husband as he."

" Enough.   I must submit to my fate—to ruin."

"Ruin! Father; what is the meaning of this? There is some secret—some danger. Trust me, dear father! Let me know what it is!"

"I may well do that, since it cannot be much longer a secret. There *is* danger, Helen—*the danger of debt.* I am in debt to the father of Richard Darke—deeply so — completely in his power. Everything I possess, land, houses, slaves, may become his at any hour; to-morrow, if he will it. Nay, he is sure to will it, now. Your little word 'No' will bring about a great change—the crisis I have been so long apprehending. Never mind! Let it come. I must meet it like a man. It is for you, dear Helen— you and Jessie, that I grieve. Poor girls, what a change in your prospects! Poverty, coarse fare, coarse garments to wear, and a log cabin to live in. Henceforth, this must be your lot. I can hope for no other."

"And what of all that, father? What care we? I, for one, do not; and I'm sure sister will say the same. But is there no way to——"

"Release me from debt, you would say? You

need not ask that. I have spent many a sleepless night over it. No; there was only that one way. I never before spoke, or even thought, of it. I knew it would not do. I knew you did not love Richard Darke, and would not consent to marry him. You could not, my child—could you ?"

Helen Armstrong did not make immediate answer; though she had one in her heart, ready to leap to her lips.

Marry Richard Darke ! Wretch; worthless, with all his riches; dissipated, wicked of soul, craven of spirit, coward as she deemed him ! Marry such a man, while another man that to her seemed possessed of every noble quality, beauty of person, boldness of spirit, purity of heart—in short, everything that makes heroism ! This other man, too, having confessed that he loved her ! To such as she it made no difference about his being poor in purse, which he was; nor would it, had he been beneath her in social rank, which he was not. Her answer would have been all the same; and she only hesitated giving it, from a thought that it might add to the weight of unhappiness at the moment pressing upon her father.

Mistaking her silence, and perhaps with the spectre of poverty before him—inciting to meanness, as it oft does the noblest natures—he said,

" Helen! could you marry him ?"

He meant Richard Darke.

" Speak ·candidly," he continued, " and take time to reflect before answering. If you think you could not be contented, happy, with him for your husband, better it should never be. Consult your own heart, my child, and do not be swayed by me or my necessities. Say, *could you marry him ?"*

" Father, I have said. You have spoken of a change in our circumstances—of poverty, and other ills. Let them come! For myself I care not. Only for you. But if to me the alternative were death, I've told you, dear father—I tell you again—I would rather that than be the wife of Richard Darke."

" Then his wife you shall never be! Let the

subject drop. Let the ruin fall! Now to prepare ourselves for poverty and Texas!"

"Texas, if you will, but not poverty. No, father, not that. The wealth of affection will make you feel rich; and in a lowly hut, as in this our grand mansion, you shall still have mine."

On saying this, the beautiful girl flung herself upon her father's breast, one hand resting upon his shoulder, the other laid caressingly on his head.

The door opened. Another entered the room —another girl, almost beautiful as herself, only a year or two younger.

"Not only *my* affection," she said, at sight of the new comer, "but Jessie's as well. Won't he, sister?"

Jessie, wondering what it was all about, nevertheless saw that something was wanted of her. She had caught the word "affection," at the same time observing the troubled expression upon her father's face. This, with her sister's attitude, decided her; and, gliding forward, in another instant she was by his side, clinging to the opposite shoulder; she too, with one hand rested gently upon his head.

Thus grouped, the three figures composed a family picture, expressive of purest love. The white-haired, white-moustached colonel, veteran of more than one campaign, in the centre; on each side a fair girl, twining alabaster arms around his neck. And yet the two different as if no kinship existed between them—Helen of gipsy darkness, Jessie bright as a summer beam.

It would have been a pleasing tableau to one who knew nothing of what had brought the three thus together; or even knowing this, to him truly comprehending it. For in the faces of all beamed affection, that bespoke well for their future, and showed no distrustful fear of either poverty or Texas.

CHAPTER III.

A FOREST POST-BOX.

EPHRAIM DARKE's harsh treatment of his slaves had the usual effect—it caused them occasionally to "abscond." Then it became necessary to insert an advertisement in the county newspaper, offering a reward for the runaways. Thus cruelty proved expensive.

In planter Darke's case, however, the cost was partially recouped by the cleverness of his son; who was a noted "nigger-catcher," and kept dogs for the especial purpose. He had a natural *penchant* for this kind of chase; and, having little else to do, passed a good deal of his time scouring the country in pursuit of his father's advertised runaways. Having caught them, he would claim the "bounty," just as if they belonged to a stranger.

Darke *père* paid it without grudge or grumbling —perhaps the only disbursement he ever made in such mood. It was like taking out of one pocket to put into the other. Besides, he was rather proud of his son's acquitting himself so shrewdly.

Skirting the two plantations, with others in the same line of settlements, was a cypress swamp. It extended along the edge of the great river, covering an area of many square miles. Besides being a swamp, it was a network of creeks, bayous, and lagoons, often inundated, and only passable by means of skiff or canoe. In most places it was a slough of soft mud, where man might not tread, nor any kind of water-craft make way. Over it, at all times, hung the obscurity of twilight. The solar rays, however bright above, could not penetrate its thick canopy of cypress tops, loaded with that strangest of parasitical plants, the *tillandsia usneoides*.

This tract of forest offered a safe place of concealment for runaway slaves; and as such was it noted throughout the neighbourhood. A "darkey" absconding from any of the near-lying plantations was as sure to make for it, as would a chased rabbit for its warren.

Sombre and gloomy though it was, around its edge was the favourite scouting-ground of Richard Darke. To him the cypress swamp was a preserve, as a coppice to the pheasant-shooter, or a scrubwood to the hunter of foxes. With the difference, that his game was human, and therefore the pursuit of it more exciting.

There were places in the swamp to which he had never penetrated—large tracts unexplored, and where exploration could not be made without much difficulty. But to enter the swamp was not absolutely necessary. The slaves, who sought asylum there, could not always remain within its gloomy recesses. Food must be obtained beyond its border, or starvation would be their fate. For this reason the refugee required some mode of communicating with the outside world. It was usually by means of a confederate —some old friend and fellow-slave upon one of the adjacent plantations—privy to the secret of his hiding-place. On this necessity the negro-catcher most depended; having often found the stalk—or "still-hunt," in backwoods phraseology —more profitable than a pursuit with trained hounds.

About a month after his rejection by Miss Armstrong, Richard Darke was out upon a chase, as usual along the edge of the cypress swamp. Rather should it be called a search : since he had found no traces of the game that had tempted him forth. This was a fugitive negro—one of the best field-hands belonging to his father's plantation—who had absconded, and could not be found.

For several weeks "Jupiter," as the runaway was called, had been missing; and his description, with the reward attached, had appeared in the county newspaper. Richard Darke, having suspicion that he was hiding somewhere in the swamp, had made several excursions thither, in the hope of lighting upon his tracks. But Jupiter was an astute fellow, and had hitherto contrived to leave no trace that could in any way contribute to his capture.

Darke was returning home, after an unsuccess-
ful day's search, in anything but a pleasant mood.
It was not so much from having failed in obtaining traces of the missing slave. That was but a
matter of money ; and, as he had plenty, the disappointment could be borne. It was the thought
of Helen Armstrong—of his scorned suit and
blighted love prospects—that gave austerity to
his reflections.

They had been further embittered by a circumstance that had since occurred. Charles Clancy
had returned from Texas. Some one had told
Darke of his being seen with Helen Armstrong—
alone. Such an interview could not have been
with her father's consent, but clandestine. So
much the more aggravating to him—Dick Darke.

He had left the swamp behind, and was
making his way through a tract of woodland
which separated his father's plantation from that
of his neighbour, when he saw something that
promised relief to his perturbed spirit. It was a
woman coming through the woods, and from the
direction of Colonel Armstrong's house.

It was not Colonel Armstrong's daughter. He did not for a moment suppose it was she. Not likely, in such a solitary place, so far from the plantation-house. But, if not the young lady herself, it was her representative—her maid—a mulatto girl named Julia. Darke recognised her at a glance, even in the far distance and under the dim shadow of the trees.

"Thank God for the devil's luck!" he muttered, as the girl first came in sight. "It's Jupiter's sweetheart; his Juno or Leda, yellow-skinned like himself. There can be no doubt about her being on the way to keep an appointment with him. No more than I shall be present at that interview. Two hundred dollars reward for old Jupe, and the fun of giving the d—d nigger a good hiding, once I have him home. Keep on, Jule, my girl! You'll track him up for me better than the best bloodhound in my kennel."

While making this soliloquy, the speaker withdrew himself behind a bush; and, concealed by its thick foliage, kept his eye on the mulatto wench, still wending her way among the tree trunks.

There was no path, and she was evidently proceeding by stealth—giving him reason to believe
she was on the errand conjectured.

Richard Darke had no doubt of her being *en
route* to an interview with Jupe; and he felt
as good as certain of soon discovering, and se-
curing, the runaway who had so long contrived
to elude him.

When the girl had passed the place of his concealment—which she soon after did—he slipped
out from behind the bush, and followed her with
stealthy tread, taking care to keep cover between
them.

It was not long before she came to a stop; under
a grand magnolia, whose spreading branches, with
their large, laurel-like leaves, shadowed a vast cir-
cumference of ground.

Darke, who had again taken stand behind some
bushes, where he had a full view of her movements, watched them with eager eyes. Two hundred dollars at stake—two hundred for himself,
fifteen hundred for his father—Jupe's market
value—no wonder he was on the alert.

What was his astonishment, on seeing the girl take a letter from her pocket, and, standing on tiptoe, drop it into a knot-hole in the magnolia!

This done, she turned her back upon the tree; and, without staying longer under its shadow, started back along the path by which she had come—evidently going home again.

The negro-catcher was not only surprised, but chagrined. A double disappointment—the anticipation of earning two hundred dollars and giving his old slave the lash—both pleasant, both foiled!

· Still remaining in concealment, he permitted the girl to go unmolested; not moving till she was quite out of his sight. There might be some secret in the letter to concern, perhaps console, him. If so, it would soon be his.

And it soon was his, though not to console him. Whatever were the contents of that epistle, so cunningly deposited, Richard Darke, on becoming acquainted with them, reeled like a drunken man, and, to save himself from falling, sought support against the tree.

After a time, recovering, he re-read the letter, and gazed at a picture—a photograph—which the envelope also enclosed.

Then from his lips came speech, low-muttered —words of fearful menace, made emphatic by an oath.

A man's name might have been heard among his mutterings. It was Charles Clancy.

As he strode away from the spot, the firm-set lips, with the angry scintillation of his eyes, told that Clancy's life was in danger.

CHAPTER IV.

A PHOTOGRAPH IN THE FOREST.

ON the third day after that when Richard Darke had abstracted the letter from the magnolia, a man was seen making his way along the edge of the cypress swamp. It was about the same hour of the evening, though the individual was altogether different. A young man, also; but unlike to Dick Darke as two men of similar age could well be to one another. In personal appearance, he was Darke's superior; in keenness of intellect, his equal; in morality, the very opposite. A figure of medium height, with limbs tersely set, and well proportioned, told of great strength; an elastic tread betokened activity; while features finely balanced, with an eagle eye and curving lips, proclaimed the possession of courage, equal to any

demand that might be made upon it. A grand
shock of waving hair, dark brown in colour, gave
the finishing touch to this fine countenance, as
does the feather to a Tyrolese hat. He who
possessed it was habited in a hunting costume;
not for the chase on horseback, but afoot. He
wore a shooting-coat of strong stuff, with short
jack-boots, and gaiters buttoned above them.
His hat was felt, with Ibis feathers for a plume.
In his hand he carried a gun, that at a glance
could be seen to be a rifle; while by his side
slouched a large dog—a cross between stag-hound
and mastiff, with a touch of the terrier commingled. Such mongrel dogs are not always
curs, but often the best for backwoods hunting,
where keenness of scent needs to be supple-
mented by strength and staunchness.

It was Charles Clancy who was thus armed
and attended. As already said, he was afoot,
walking by the side of the cypress swamp. It
was about two weeks after his return from Texas.
He had come back to find himself fatherless; and
since had stayed much at home, to console his sor-

rowing mother. Only now and then had he gone forth to seek relaxation in the chase, and only on short excursions through the nearest tract of woodland. On this occasion he was returning with an empty game-bag; but in no way chagrined by his ill-success. For he had something else to console him; that which gave gladness to his heart—joy of the sweetest. She who had won that heart—Helen Armstrong—loved him. She had not told him so much in words; but there had been acts equally expressive, and to the full as convincing. They had met clandestinely, and in the same way corresponded; a tree in the forest serving them for post-office. All this through fear of her father. In the letters thus surreptitiously exchanged, only phrases of friendship had passed between them. But at their last meeting, Clancy had spoken words of love—fervent love, in its last appeal. He had avowed himself hers, and asked her to be his. She had resisted giving him an answer upon the spot, but promised it in writing. He would receive it in a letter, to be found in their forest post-office.

He was not dismayed at being thus put off. He supposed it to be but a whim of his sweet-heart. He knew that, like the Anne Hathaway of Shakespeare, Helen Armstrong "had a way" of her own; for she was a girl of no ordinary character. Born and brought up in the backwoods, she possessed a spirit, free and independent, in keeping with the scenes and people that had surrounded her youth. So far from being deterred by her refusal to give him an immediate answer, Clancy but admired her the more. A proud she-eagle, that would not condescend to the soft cooing of the dove—even to speak acquiescence.

This would come in time—in a way not common—in the letter she had promised him. He would find that in the knot-hole of the magnolia.

And now, his day's hunting done, he was making his way for the tract of woodland in which stood the tree—proceeding towards it along the edge of the swamp.

He had no thought of stopping, or turning aside; nor would he have done so for any small game. But at that moment a deer—a grand antlered stag—hove in sight, heading in towards the swamp. Before Clancy could bring the gun to his shoulder, it passed the place where he stood, lopping on among the trunks of the trees. As it ran apparently unscared, he had hopes of again getting sight of it; and thus allured, he swerved out of his track, and went stalking after.

He had not proceeded above twenty paces, when a sound filled his ears, as well as the woods around. It was the report of a gun fired by some one almost beside him. And not at the deer, but himself! The shot came from behind, and he knew it had hit him. This, from a stinging sensation in his arm, like the touch of red-hot iron, or a drop of scalding water. Even then he might not have known it to be a bullet, but for the crack close following.

The wound — fortunately but a slight one — did not disable him. Like a tiger stung by javelins, he was round in an instant, ready to return the fire. There was no one in sight!

As there had been no warning —not a word—

he could have no doubt of the intent: some one
meant to murder him !

The report was that of a smoothbore—a fowling-piece loaded with ball. A conclusion quickly
drawn hindered him from having any conjecture
as to who had fired the shot, or why it had been
fired. He was not travelling on a road fre-
quented by robbers, but through a track of timber in the Mississippi Bottom. He was sure of
its being an attempt to assassinate him, and that
there was but one man in the world capable of
making it. Richard Darke was in his thoughts,
as if the report of the gun had been a voice
pronouncing his name.

Clancy's eyes, flashing angrily, interrogated the
forest. The trees stood thick, the spaces between shadowy and sombre. For it was a forest
of cypresses, and the hour twilight.

He could see nothing but the tree-trunks and
their branches, garlanded with the ghostly tillandsia, here and there draping to the ground.
It baffled him, by its colour and form—the grey
festoonery having a resemblance to ascending

smoke. He was looking for the smoke of the discharged gun.

He could see none. It must have puffed up suddenly to the tree-tops, and become commingled with the moss.

It did not matter much. Neither the darkness, nor the close-standing trunks, hindered his dog from discovering the whereabouts of the would-be assassin. Giving a yelp, the animal sprang out, and off.

Before going twenty paces from the spot, it brought up aside the trunk of a tree, and there stood fiercely baying as if at a bear. The tree was a huge buttressed cypress, with " knees " several feet in height rising around. In the obscurity they might have been mistaken for men.

Clancy was soon among them ; and saw standing, between two pilasters, the man who had meant to murder him.

There could be no question about the intent; and the motive was equally understood.

There was no effort at explanation. Clancy called for none. His rifle was already cocked ;

and, quick upon the identification of his adversary, came to his shoulder.

"Richard Darke!" he cried, "you've had the first shot. It's my turn now."

As he spoke his finger pressed the trigger, and the bullet sped.

Darke, on seeing himself discovered, leaped out from his lurking-place to obtain more freedom of action. The buttresses hindered him from having elbow room. He also raised his gun—a double barrel; but, thinking it too late, instead of pulling trigger he lowered the piece again, and dodged back behind the tree. His movement, almost simultaneous with Clancy's shot, was quick enough to save him. The ball passed through the skirt of his coat, without drawing blood, or even creasing his skin.

He sprang out again with a shout of triumph, his gun still cocked and ready.

Deliberately bringing the butt against his shoulder—for he was now sure of his victim—he said, in a derisive tone,

"You're a clumsy fellow, Clancy! A sorry

marksman, to miss a man not six feet from the muzzle of your gun! I shan't miss you. Shot for shot's fair play. I've had the first, and I'll have the last. Now, take your *death shot !*"

As he saw the words, a fiery jet streamed from his left-hand barrel.

For the moment Clancy was invisible, the sulphureous smoke forming a nimbus around him. When it ascended, he was seen prostrate upon the earth ; the blood, welling from a wound in his breast, having already saturated his shirt !

He appeared to be writhing in his death agony.

He must have thought so himself, from the words that came through his lips, in slow, choking utterance,

" May God forgive you, Richard Darke—you have killed,—murdered me ?"

" I meant to do it," was the unpitying response.

 " Oh Heavens ! — wicked wretch — why — why——"

" Bah ! You know the why, well enough.

Helen Armstrong, if you like to hear it. After all, it wasn't that's made me kill you ; but your impudence, thinking you had a chance with her. You hadn't ; she never cared a straw for you. Perhaps, before dying, it may be a consolation for you to know she never did. I've got the proof. Since it's not likely you'll ever see herself again, it may give you a pleasure to look at her portrait. Here it is ! The sweet girl sent it me this very morning, with her autograph attached, as you see. I think it an excellent likeness. What think you ? You will, no doubt, give an unbiassed opinion. One in your condition should speak candidly."

The ruffian held a photograph before the eyes of the dying man. They were growing dim ; but only death could have dimmed them, so as not to see that sun-painted picture, the portrait of her he loved.

He gazed upon it lovingly, but not long. The script underneath claimed his attention. In it he recognised her handwriting known to him. The fear of death itself was naught to the despair that swept through his soul, as, with fast-filming eyes, he deciphered the words—

" *Helen Armstrong.—For him she loves.* "

The picture was in the possession of Richard Darke. To Darke, then, had the words been addressed.

" The sweet creature !" repeated the latter, pouring the bitter speech into his victim's ear. " She sent it me this very morning. Come, Clancy! tell me what you think of the likeness ?"

There was no response—neither by word, look, nor gesture. Clancy's lips were mute ; his eyes glassed over ; his body motionless as the mud on which it lay.

" D——n him he's dead !"

CHAPTER V.

UNDER THE CYPRESS.

"D——N him, he's dead!"

It was Richard Darke who gave utterance to the speech, blasphemous as brutal.

Profanity and brutality had been the characteristics of his life. To these he had now added a crime of deeper dye—murder.

And without remorse. As he bent over the lifeless form of his rival there was no resemblance of contrition, either in glance or gesture. On the contrary, his dark animal eyes were still sparkling with jealous hate, while his hand clutched the hilt of his bowie-knife. He had half drawn it from its sheath, as if to plunge it into the body. He saw it was already breathless—almost bloodless.

" What need ?   The man's dead."

And, with this reflection, he pushed the blade back.

Now for the first time a thought of danger flashed across his brain. A sense of fear began to shape itself in his soul. For, beyond doubt, he had done murder !

" No !" he said, in an attempt at self-justification.   " It's no murder.   I've killed him, that's true; but he's had a shot at me.   I can show that his gun is discharged, and here's his bullet-hole through the skirt of my coat.   By thunder, it was a close shave !"

His eyes rested for a moment on the perforated skirt—only a moment. His uneasiness came back, and he continued to shape self-excuses.

" Bah !   It was a fair fight.   The thing happens every day in the streets.   What difference whether it's among trees or houses ?   What difference — only that there were no witnesses ? Well, what if there were none ?"

The assassin stood reflecting—his glance now bent upon the body, now sent searchingly through the trees, as if afraid that some one might come along.

There was not much danger of this. The spot was one of perfect solitude, as is always a cypress forest. There was no path near, to be trodden by the wayfarer. The planter had no business among those great buttressed trunks. The woodman could never assail them with his axe. Only a stalking hunter, or perhaps some runaway slave, would be likely to stray thither.

Richard Darke soliloquised as follows :—

" Shall I put a bold face upon it, and confess that I killed him ? I can say we met while out hunting; that it's been a fair fight—shot for shot; my luck to have the last. Will that story stand ?"

A pause in the soliloquy; a glance at the corpse; another that interrogated the surrounding scene, taking in the huge unshapely trunks, the long outstretched limbs, with their pall-like festoonery of Spanish moss; a thought about the loneliness of the place; its fitness for concealing a dead body; then a reflection as to the social status of the man he had murdered. All these passed through the mind of the murderer, diverting him from his half-formed resolution—admonishing him of its futility.

"It won't do," he went on, his words denoting the change. "No, that it won't! Better say nothing about him. He has no friends who'll inquire what's become of him; only his old mother. 'As for Helen Armstrong, will she—Ach!"

The ejaculation betrayed extreme acerbity of spirit, as if called up by the name. Strange, with such a sweet love-token lying along his breast!

He again glanced inquiringly round, this time with a view to secreting the corpse. He had made up his mind to do this.

A sluggish creak meandered among the trees, passing at some two hundred yards from the spot. At about a like-distance below, it discharged itself into the stagnant reservoirs of the swamp.

Its waters were dark, from the overshadowing

of the cypresses, and deep enough for such a purpose as he was planning.

But to carry the body to it would require an effort of strength; and to drag it would leave traces.

In view of this difficulty, he said to himself:

"I'll let it stay where it is. No one ever comes this way; not likely. It may lie there till doomsday, or till the wolves and buzzards make bare bones of it. Then who can tell whose bones they are? Ah! better still, I'll throw some of this moss over it, and scatter more around. That will hide everything."

He rested his gun against a tree, and commenced dragging the beard-like parasite from the branches above. It came off in flakes—in armfuls. Half a dozen he flung over the still palpitating corpse; then pitched on the top some pieces of dead wood, lest a stray breeze might strip off the hoary shroud.

After strewing some tufts around, to conceal the blood and boot tracks, he stood for a time making survey of the scene.

At length satisfied, he again laid hold of his gun, and was about taking departure from the place; when a sound, falling upon his ear, caused him to start. Well was it calculated to do so: for it was as the voice of one wailing for the dead!

At first he was badly scared, but got over it on discovering the cause.

"Only the dog!" he said, as he saw Clancy's deerhound skulking among the trees.

On its master being shot down the animal had scampered off, perhaps fearing a similar fate. It had not gone far, and was now returning— little by little, drawing nearer to the spot.

The poor brute was struggling between two instincts—affection for its fallen master, and fear for its own life.

As Darke's gun was now empty, he tried to entice the creature within reach of his knife.

With all his wheedling, it would not come.

Hastily ramming a cartridge into one of the barrels, he took aim at the animal, and fired.

The shot had effect; the ball passing through

4—2

the fleshy part of the dog's neck. But only to crease the skin and draw out a spurt of blood. The animal, stung and still further affrighted, gave out a wild howl, and went off, without sign of stay or return.

Equally wild were the words that proceeded from the lips of the assassin, as he stood looking after. They were interrogative.

"The d——d cur 'll go home to the house? He'll tell a tale—perhaps guide people to the spot?"

As he spoke, the murderer turned pale. It was the first time he had experienced real fear. In such an out-of-the-way place he had felt safe about concealing the body, and along with it his bloody deed. Then, he had not taken the dog into account, and the odds were in his favour. But now, with the animal adrift, they were heavily against him.

It needed no calculation of chances to make this clear. Nor was it a doubt which caused him to stand hesitating. His irresolution came partly from affright, partly from uncertainty as to what course he should pursue.

One thing was certain — he could not stay there. The hound had gone off *howling*. It was two miles to the nearest plantation house; but there was an odd squatter's cabin and clearing between. A dog going in that guise, blood-bedraggled, and in full cry of distress, would be certain to raise an alarm. Equally certain to beget apprehensions for the safety of its missing master, and cause search to be made.

Richard Darke did not long stand thinking. Despite its solitude, it was not the place for tranquil thought—not for him. Far off through the trees he could hear the wail of the wounded Molossian. Was it fancy, or did he also hear men's voices ?

He stayed not to ascertain. Beside ,that corpse, shrouded though it was, he dared not remain a moment longer.

Hastily shouldering his gun, he struck off through the forest; at first going in quick step; then in double; increasing to a run, impelled to this speed not by the howls of the hound, but the fancy that he heard human voices.

He retreated in a direction opposite to that taken by the dog. It was also opposite to the way leading to his father's house. It forced him still further into the swamp—across sloughs and through soft mud, where he made foot-marks. Though he had carefully concealed the body, and obliterated all other traces of the strife, in his "scare" he did not think of those he was now leaving.

The murderer is only cunning before the crime. After it, if he have conscience—or rather, having not courage and coolness—he loses self-possession, and is sure to leave clues for the detective.

So was it with Richard Darke. As he retreated from the scene of his diabolical deed, taking long strides, his only thought was to put space between himself and that accursed crying cur. So he anathematised the animal, whose cries appeared commingling with the shouts of men— the voices of avengers!

CHAPTER VI.

A COON-CHASE INTERRUPTED.

THERE is no district in the Southern States without its noted coon-hunter. And, notedly, the coon-hunter is a negro. The pastime is too tame, or too humble, to tempt the white man. Sometimes the sons of "poor white trash" take part in it; but it is usually delivered over to the "darkey."

In the old times of slavery every plantation could boast of one or more of these sable Nimrods. To them coon-catching was a profit, as well as a sport; the skins keeping them in tobacco—and whisky, when addicted to drinking it. The flesh, too, though little esteemed by white palates, was a *bonne-bouche* to the negro, with whom flesh meat was a scarce commodity. It often furnished him with the means of making a savoury roast.

The plantation of Ephraim Darke was no exception to the general rule. It, too, had its coon-hunter—a negro named, or nicknamed, " Blue Bill." The qualifying term came from a cerulean tinge, that in certain lights appeared upon the surface of his sable epidermis. Otherwise he was black as ebony.

Blue Bill was a mighty hunter of his kind, passionately fond of the coon-chase—too much, indeed, for his own safety and comfort. It carried him abroad, when the discipline of the plantation required him to be at home; and more than once, for so absenting himself, had his shoulders been scored by the lash.

All this had not cured him of his proclivity. Unluckily for Richard Darke, it had not. For on the evening of Clancy's being shot down, as described, Blue Bill was abroad; and, with a small cur which he had trained to his favourite chase, was ranging the woods near the edge of the cypress swamp.

He had "treed" an old he-coon; and was pre-
paring to climb up to the creature's nest—a large
knot-hole in a sycamore—when a shot startled
him. He was more disturbed by the peculiar
crack, than by the fact of its being the report of
a gun. His ear, accustomed to the sound, knew
it to have proceeded from the double-barrel belonging to his young master—just then the last
man he would have wished to meet. He was
away from the "quarter" without "pass" or
permission of any kind.

His first thought was to continue his ascent of
the sycamore, and conceal himself among its
branches.

But his dog, still upon the ground—that would
betray him ?

While hurriedly reflecting on what he had best
do, he heard a second shot. Then a third, coming
quickly after; while mingling with the reports
were men's voices, apparently in angry expostu-
lation. He heard, too, the baying of a hound.

"Gorramity!" muttered Blue Bill; "dar's a
skrimmage goin' on dar—a fight, I reck'n, to de

def! And I know who dat fight's between. De
fuss shot am Mass' Dick's gun; de oder am Mass'
Charle Clancy. By golly! 'taint safe dis child be
seed hya, no how. Whar kin a hide maseff?"

Again he looked upward, scanning the sycamore; then down at his dog; and once more to
the trunk of the tree. It was embraced by a
creeper—a gigantic grape-vine—up which an
ascent might easily be made; so easily that there
need be no difficulty in the carrying his cur along
with him. It was the ladder he had intended
using to reach the treed coon. With the fear of
his young master coming that way, and if so,
surely "cowhiding" him, he felt there was no
time to be wasted in vacillation.

Nor did he waste any. Without further stay,
he threw his arm around the coon-dog; raised the
unresisting animal from the ground; and then
"swarmed" up the creeper, like a she-bear carrying her cub.

In ten seconds after, he was ensconced in a
crotch of the sycamore; safely screened from the
observation of anyone who might pass under-

neath, by the profuse clustering foliage of the parasite.

Feeling comparatively secure, he bent his ears more attentively to listen. He still heard two voices in conversation. Then only one of them, as if the other no longer replied. The one continuing to speak he could distinguish as that of his young master; though he could not make out the words spoken. The distance was too great, and the sound interrupted by the thick-standing trunks. It was a low monotone—might have been a soliloquy—and ended in an ejaculation. Even this he could only tell by its abrupt terminating tone.

Then succeeded a short interval of silence, as if both men had gone away. Blue Bill was in hopes they had, or that his young master might have done so. His hope was the stronger, that the tree in which he had secreted himself was not upon the way Richard Darke should take, returning to the plantation. It was night; and naturally he would be going home.

While thus reflecting, the coon-hunter's ear

was again saluted by a sound. This time it was
the hound that spoke—not barking as before, but
in a low, lugubrious wail, a sort of whimper,
which appeared to come from a direction different. Then again the voice of a man—Massa
Dick's—who spoke as if coaxing the animal, and
calling it up.

Another short interval of silence. Another
shot, succeeded by an angry exclamation. Then
the hound was heard in continuous howling,
which · gradually grew more indistinct, as if the
animal was going off on the opposite side.

To the slave, absent without leave, all these
sounds seemed ominous—indicative of some tragical occurrence. As he sat in the fork of the
sycamore, listening to them, he trembled like an
aspen leaf. Still, his presence of mind did not
forsake him; and this was directed to keeping
his own dog silent. Hearing the hound, the cur
might give tongue in response—perhaps would
have done so, but for the coon-hunter's fingers
clasped chokingly round its throat, and only de-
tached to give it an occasional cuff.

Once more stillness held possession of the forest. But again was it disturbed by the tread of footsteps, and a swishing among the underwood. Some one was passing through it, evidently making towards the tree where the coon-hunter was concealed.

More than ever Blue Bill trembled upon his perch; tighter than ever clutching the throat of his canine companion. For he felt sure the man, whose footsteps told of approach, was his master—or rather his master's son. They told also that he was advancing hastily; as if in retreat, rapid, headlong, confused. Upon this the peccant slave founded hopes of escaping observation, and consequent chastisement.

The sign did not disappoint him. In a few seconds after, he saw Richard Darke coming from the direction in which the shots and voices had been heard. He was running as for very life—the more like it, that he ran crouchingly, at intervals making stop, and standing to listen, with chin thrown back upon his shoulder!

When opposite the sycamore—almost under it

—he made a pause longer than the others. The sweat appeared pouring down his cheeks, over his eyebrows, almost blinding him.

He drew a handkerchief from his coat-pocket; wiped it off; and then, replacing the kerchief, ran on again.

In doing this, he dropped something, unseen by himself. It did not escape the observation of the coon-hunter, conspicuously posted. The thing let fall resembled a letter, in an envelope of the ordinary kind.

This it proved to be, when Blue Bill, cautiously descending from the sycamore, approached the spot where it had fallen, and picked it up.

The coon-hunter could not read. No use his taking out the letter, though he saw that the envelope was open. But an instinct that it might, in some way or at some time, be useful, prompted him to put it in his pocket.

This done, he stood reflecting. There was now no sound to disturb him. The footsteps of Richard Darke were no longer heard. Their tread, gradually growing indistinct, had died away; the cypress forest resuming its pristine silence. The only sound the coon-hunter heard was the thumping of his own heart against his ribs—this loud enough.

No longer thought he of the coon he had succeeded in treeing. The animal, late devoted to certain death, would owe its escape to an accident, and might now repose securely within its nest. Blue Bill had other thoughts—emotions strong enough to drive coon-hunting clean out of his head. Among them were apprehensions about his own safety. Though unseen by his young master—his presence even unsuspected —he knew that an unlucky chance had placed him in a position of danger. Of this his instinct had already warned him.

That a tragedy had been enacted, he not only surmised, but was pretty sure of.

Under the circumstances, how was he to act? Go on to the place where he had heard the shots, and ascertain what had actually occurred?

At first he thought of doing this; but soon changed the intention. Frightened at what was already known to him, he dared not know more. His young master might be a murderer? The way in which he saw him retreating almost said he was. Was he, Blue Bill, to make himself acquainted with the crime, and bear witness against the man who had committed it? As a slave, he knew that his testimony would count for nothing in a court of justice. And as the slave of Ephraim Darke, he also knew his life would not be worth much, after he had given it.

This last reflection decided him; and, still carrying the coon-dog under his arm, he parted from the spot, going in skulking gait, never stopping, never feeling safe, till he found himself within the limits of the " negro quarter."

Not then, till inside his own cabin, seated by the side of his Phœbe, his coon-dog smelling among the pots, and his "piccaninnies" clustering around, and clambering upon his knees.

CHAPTER VII.

THE ASSASSIN IN RETREAT.

ATHWART the thick timber, going as one pursued —in a track straight as the underwood allows— at times breaking through it like a chased bear— now stumbling over a fallen log, or caught in a trailing grape-vine—Richard Darke flees from the place where he has laid his rival low.

He makes neither stop nor stay; if so, only for a few instants at a time, long enough to listen and try to discover whether he is followed.

Whether or not, he fancies it; again starting off, with terror in his looks and trembling in his limbs. The *sang-froid* he had exhibited while in the act of concealing the body has quite forsaken him now. Then he felt confident there could be no witness of the deed—nothing to connect him with it as the doer. It was the un-thought-of presence of the dog that produced the change, or, rather, the thought of the animal having escaped. This, and his own frightened fancies; for he is now really in affright.

He keeps on for quite a mile in headlong, reckless rushing. Then, as fatigue overtakes him, his terror becomes less impulsive; his fancies freer from exaggeration; and, believing himself far enough from the scene of danger, he at length desists from flight.

He sits down upon a log, draws forth his pocket-handkerchief, and wipes the sweat from his face. He is panting, palpitating, perspiring at every pore. But he now finds time to reflect; and his first reflection is the absurdity of his precipitate retreat; his next, its imprudence.

"I've been a fool for it," he mutters. "Supposing some one had seen me? 'Twould only have made things worse.

"And what have I been running from? Only a hound, and nothing besides. D—n the dog! Let him go home, and be hanged! He can't tell a tale upon me. The scratch of a bullet—who could say what sort of ball, or what kind of gun it came from? No danger in that, and I've been stupid to think there could be.

"Well, it's all over now; and here I am. What next?"

For some minutes he remains upon the log, with the gun resting across his knees, and his head bent down between them. He appears engaged in some abstruse calculation. Something new is evidently before his mind—some scheme requiring all his power of thought to elaborate.

"*I* shall keep that tryst," he says, seeming at length to have settled it. "Yes; *I* shall meet her under the magnolia. Who can tell what changes may be brought about in the heart of a woman? In history I had a royal namesake—a king of England with a hump on his shoulders — as he's said himself, ' deformed, unfinished, sent into the world scarce half made up,' so that the ' dogs barked at him,' as this brute of Clancy's has been doing at me. And this royal Richard, shaped ' so lamely and unfashionable,' made court to her

whose husband he had just assassinated — a
proud Queen—wooed and subdued her! Surely,
this should encourage me? The more that I,
Richard Darke, am neither halt nor humpbacked.
No, nor yet unfashionable, as many a pretty girl
has said, and more than one sworn it.

"Proud, Helen Armstrong may be; proud as
Queen Anne she is. For all that, I've got something may subdue her—a scheme as cunning as
that of my royal namesake. May God, or the
Devil, grant me a like success!"

At the moment of giving utterance to the pro-
fane prayer, he starts to his feet. Then, taking
out his watch, consults it as to the time.

"Half-past nine it is now. Ten was the hour
of appointment. There won't be time for me to
go home, and then over to Armstrong's wood-
ground. It's more than two miles from this. No
matter about going home. There's no need to
change my dress; she won't notice this tear in
the skirt. If she should, she'd never think of
what had caused it, much less it's being a bullet.
She won't see it anyhow. I must be off. It will

never do to keep a young lady waiting. If she don't feel disappointed at seeing me, bless her! If she do, I say curse her! What's passed prepares me for either event. In any case, I shall have satisfaction for the slight she's put upon me. By G—d I'll get that!"

He is stepping off when a thought occurs to him. He is not certain as to the exact hour of the tryst. He might be there too late. To make sure, he plunges his hand into the pocket, where he had deposited both letter and photograph, after holding the latter before the eyes of the dying man, and witnessing the fatal effect. With all his diabolical hardihood, he had been a little awed by this, and had thrust the papers into his pocket hastily, carelessly.

They are no longer there! Neither letter nor photograph can be found!

He tries the other pockets of his dress—all of them—with like result. He examines his bullet-pouch and game-bag. No letter, no cardboard, not a scrap of paper in either! The stolen epistle, its envelope, the inclosure, all are absent.

After once more ransacking his pockets, almost turning them inside out, he comes to the conclusion that the precious papers are lost.

It startles, and for a moment dismays him. Where is the missing epistle? He must have let it fall while retreating through the trees.

Shall he go back in search of it?

No; he will not. He does not dare to return upon that track. The forest path is too sombre, too solitary, now. By the margin of the dank lagoon, under the ghostly shadow of the cypresses, he might meet the ghost of Charles Clancy!

And why should he go back? After all, there is no need. What is there in the letter requiring him to regain possession of it? Nothing that can in any way compromise him. Why, then, should he care to recover it?

" Let the d——d thing go to the devil, and the picture too! Let them rot where they've fallen — I suppose in the mud, or among the palmettoes. No matter for that. But it does matter, my being under the magnolia in good time. I must stay no longer here."

Obedient to the resolution thus formed, he re-buttons his coat, cast open in the search for the missing papers; throws his double-barrel—the murder-gun—over his shoulder; and strides off to keep an appointment not made for him, but for the man he has murdered!

CHAPTER VIII.

THE COON-HUNTER AT HOME.

THERE was yet a lingering ray of daylight in the cleared ground of Ephraim Darke's plantation, as Blue Bill, returning from his interrupted chase, got back to the negro quarter. He had entered it, as already told, with stealthy tread, and looking cautiously around him.

For he knew that some of his fellow-slaves were aware of his having gone out " a-cooning," and would wonder at his early return—too early to pass without observation. If seen by them he might be asked for an explanation; which he was not prepared to give.

This it was that caused him to skulk in among the cabins; still carrying the dog under his arm, lest the latter might take a fancy to go scenting among the utensils of some other darkey's kitchen, and so betray his presence in the "quarter."

Fortunately for the coon-hunter, the little "shanty" that claimed him as its tenant stood at the outward extremity of the row of cabins—nearest the path leading to the plantation woodland. He was therefore enabled to reach, and re-enter it, without much danger of attracting observation.

And as it chanced, he was not observed; but got back into the bosom of his family, without anyone being a bit the wiser.

Blue Bill's domestic circle consisted of his wife, Phœbe, and several half-naked little "niggers." Once more among them, however, he found he was still not safe, but had yet a gauntlet to run. His re-appearance so soon, unexpected; his empty game-bag; the coon-dog carried under his arm; all had their effect upon Phœbe. She could not help having a surprise.

Nor did she submit to it in silence.

Confronting her dark-skinned lord and master, with arms set akimbo, she said:—

"Bress de Lor', Bill! Wha' for you so soon home? Neider coon nor possum! An' de dog toated after dat fashun! You ain't been a gone more 'n a hour! Who'd speck see you come back dat-a way, empy handed; nuffin, 'cep your own ole dog! 'Splain it, Bill?"

The coon-hunter dropped his canine companion to the floor, and saté down upon a stool, but without giving the demanded explanation. He only said:—

"Nebba mind, Phœbe gal; nebba you mind why I'se home so soon. Dat's nuffin 'trange. I seed de night warn't a gwine to be fav'ble fo' trackin' de coon; so dis nigga konklood ter leab ole cooney 'lone."

"Lookee hya, Bill!" said his wife, laying her hand upon his shoulder, and gazing earnestly into his eyes. "Dat ere ain't de correck explicashun. Yer ain't tellin' me de troof!"

The coon-hunter quailed under the searching glance, as if in reality a criminal; but gave no response. He was at a loss what answer to make.

" Da's somethin' mysteerus 'bout dis," continued his better half. " You've got a seecrit,
nigga; I kin tell it by de glint ob yer eye. I
nebba see dat look on ye, but I know you ain't
yaseff; jess as ye use deseeve me, when you war
in sich a way 'bout brown Bet."

" Wha you talkin 'bout, Phœbe ? Dar's no
brown Bet in de case. I swar dar ain't."

" Who sayed dar war ? No, Bill, dat's all pass.
I only spoked ob her 'kase yar look jess now
like ye did when Bet used bamboozle ye. What
I say now am dat you ain't yaseff. Dar's a cat in
de bag, somewha; you better let her out, and
confess de whole 'tory."

As Phœbe made this appeal, her glance rested
searchingly upon her husband's face, and keenly
scrutinised the play of his features.

There was not much play to be observed. The
coon-hunter was a pure-blooded African, with features immobile as those of the Sphinx. And from
his colour nought could be deduced. As already
said, it was the purity of its ebon blackness,
producing a purplish iridescence over the epi-

dermis, that had gained for him the sobriquet of
" Blue Bill."

Unflinchingly he stood the inquisitorial glance;
and for the time Phœbe was foiled.

Only until after supper, when the frugality of
the meal—made so by the barren chase—had
perhaps something to do in melting his heart, and
relaxing his tongue.   Whether this, or whatever
the cause, certain it is, that before going to bed,
he unburdened himself to the partner of his joys,
by making full confession of what he had wit-
nessed on the swamp edge.

He told her, also, of the letter he had picked
up ; which, cautiously pulling out of his pocket,
he handed over for her inspection.

Phœbe had once been a family servant—an
indoor domestic and handmaiden to a white
mistress.   This was in the days of youth—the
halcyon days of girlhood, in " Ole Varginny "—
before she had been transported west, sold to
Ephraim Darke, and by him degraded to the lot
of an ordinary outdoor slave.   But her original
owner had taught her to " read," and her memory

still retained a trace of this early education—
sufficient for her to decipher the script she now
held in her hands.

She first looked at the photograph; as it came
first out of the envelope. There could be no
mistaking whose portrait it was. Helen Armstrong was too conspicuously beautiful to have
escaped the notice of the humblest slave in the
settlement. Too good, also; for, as a friend to
the black folks, she was known to them throughout the whole line of riverine plantations.

The negress spent some minutes gazing upon
the fair face, as she did so remarking:—

" How bewful am dat young lady! What pity
she gwine away from de place !"

" You am right 'bout dat, Phœbe. She bewful
as any white gal dis nigga ebber sot eyes on.
And she good as bewful. I'se sorry she gwine
'way from dese parts. How many a darkie 'll
miss dat dear young lady. An' won't Mass
Charl Clancy miss her too! Lor! I most for-
got; maybe he no trouble 'bout her now;
maybe he's gone dead! Ef dat so, she miss

him, an' no mistake. She cry her eyes out, shoo-satin."

"You tink dar war someting 'tween dem two ?"

"Tink ! I'se shoo ob dat, Phœbe. Didn't I see dem boaf togedder down dar in de woodland, when I war out a coon-huntin'. More'n once I seed em. A young white lady an' genl'm don't meet dat way unless dar's a feelin' atween em, any more dan we poor brack folks. Besides, dis nigga know dey lub one noder—he know fo satin. Jule, she tell Jupe; and Jupe hab trussed dat same seecret to me. Dey been in lub long time; afore Mass Charl went 'way to Texas. But de great Kurnel Armtrong, he don't know nuffin' 'bout it. Golly ! ef he did, he shoo kill Charl Clancy; dat is, if de poor young man ain't dead arready. Le's hope 'taint so. But, Phœbe, gal, open dat letter, an' see what de young lady say. Satin it's been wrote by her. Maybe it trow some light on dis dark subjeck."

Phœbe, thus requested, took the letter out of the envelope. Then spreading it out and holding it close to the flare of the tallow dip, read it from beginning to end.

It took a considerable time; as her scholastic acquirements, not very bright at the best, had become dimmed by long disuse. For all, she succeeded in deciphering and interpreting every item of its contents to the coon-hunter; who sate listening with eyes in wonderment, and ears wide open.

When finished, and the letter, along with the photograph, was replaced in the envelope, the two were for some time silent, pondering upon the circumstances thus revealed to them.

Blue Bill was the first to resume speech. He said :—

"Dar's a good deal in dat letter I know'd afore, and dar's odder points as 'pear to be new to me; but whether de old or de new, 'twon't do for you or me to declar a single word o' what de young lady hab say. No, Phœbe, neery word must 'scape de lips ob eider o' us. We muss hide de letter, an' neber let nob'dy know dar's sich a dockyment in our poseshun. And dar must be nuffin' sayed or know'd 'bout dis nigga findin' it. Ef dat ebber kum out, den I needn't tell you what 'ud happen to us. We'd boaf catch de cow-hide, an' maybe de punishment ob de pump. So, Phœbe, gal, gi'e me yar promise to keep dark, for de case am a desprit one."

Phœbe could well comprehend the caution; and promising compliance, the two went to sleep by the side of their sable offspring, resolved on preserving silence.

CHAPTER IX.

UNDER THE MAGNOLIA.

PERHAPS for the first time in her life, Helen Armstrong walked with stealthy step, and crouchingly. Daughter of a large slave-owner—mistress over many slaves—she was accustomed to an upright attitude and aristocratic bearing. But she was now on an errand that required more than ordinary caution, and would dread recognition by the humblest slave on her father's estate.

Cloaked and hooded—the hood drawn well over her face—with body bent, as she moved silently forward, it would have taken a sharp darkey to indentify her as his young mistress— the eldest daughter of his " Massa," Colonel Armstrong—more especially as it was after night she was thus cautiously proceeding, and under the shadow of trees.

Notwithstanding the obscurity, she was keeping in a direct course, as if making for some point, and with a purpose.

Does it need to be told what this purpose was ? Love alone could tempt a young lady out at that hour ; and only love not allowed—perhaps forbidden, by some one having ascendancy over her. Only this could account for her making her way through the wood in such secret guise.

At the same hour and moment Colonel Armstrong was at work, with all his household, white retainers as well as black slaves. Of the last there were not many left him—Ephraim Darke having foreclosed the mortgage, and obtained possession of the estate, made over to him by private sale. Three or four field hands, and some half-dozen house servants—whose affection made them almost members of his family—were all that remained to the ruined planter.

He was about to move off with these, to make the beginning of a new home in Texas ; and the next morning was appointed for starting. At an early hour, too ; so that the night was being given to the final settlement of affairs and preparation for the journey. Thus, fully occupied, chiefly with out-door matters, he had no time to give to his family. His two daughters he supposed to be equally engrossed with those cares, on such occasions, left to the female members of the household.

Had the proud planter—still proud, though now in comparative poverty — had he at that moment been told that his eldest born was abroad in the woods, it would have startled him. Further informed as to her errand—the keeping of a love appointment—it would have caused him to desist from his preparations for travel—perhaps thrown him into a terrible rage. And, still better acquainted with the circumstances—told who was the man thus favoured with a nocturnal assignation, and that it was his own daughter, his eldest, the pride of his house and heart, who had made it—it is just possible he would have dropped whatever duty he was engaged upon sprung to his pistols, and rushed off to the woods, on the track of his straying child ; there, perhaps, to enact a tragedy sanguinary as the one recounted, if not so repulsive.

Fortunately, he had no knowledge of aught that was passing. Engrossed in the cares of the night—the last he was to spend on his old plantation—thinking only of preparations for the new home—he had no suspicion of Helen being absent from the house. He saw Jessie there ; and she, her sister's *confidante*—both as to the absence and its cause—took pains to conceal both.

      *   *   *   *

Still stooping in her gait—casting furtive interrogatory glances to right, to left, forward, and behind—at intervals stopping to listen—Helen Armstrong continues on in her nocturnal excursion.

She has not far to go—half a mile or so from the house. On the edge of the cultivated ground, where the primeval forest meets the maize-field, stands a grand magnolia, that has been respected

by the woodman's axe. This is to be the tryst-
ing-tree. She knows it—she has herself named
it. It is the same tree in the knot-hole of which
her trusted maid " Jule " had deposited the letter
containing her photograph.

As she comes to a stop under its spreading
branches, she throws open her cloak, tosses the
hood back, and stands with uncovered face.

She has no fear now. The place is beyond the
range of night-strolling negroes. Only one in
pursuit of 'possum, or 'coon, would be likely to
come that way. But this is a contingency too
rare to give her uneasiness.

With features set in expectation, she stands
under the tree — within the darkness of its
shadow. Alone the fireflies illuminate her face ;
though it is one deserving a better light. But
seen, even under the pale, fitful coruscation of
the "lightning bugs,"—so coarsely, as inappro-
priately, named—its beauty is beyond cavil or
question. Black hair, black eyes and eyebrows,
complexion of golden brown, features of gipsy
type—to which the hooded cloak adds character-

istic expression—all combine in forming a picture appropriate to its framing, the forest.

Only for a few short moments does she remain motionless. Just long enough to get back her breath, spent by some exertion in making her way through the wood—more difficult in the darkness. Strong emotions, too, contribute to the quick beating of her heart.

She does not wait for it to be stilled. Facing towards the tree, and standing on tiptoe, she raises her hand aloft, and commences groping against the trunk. The fireflies gleam on her slender snow-white fingers, as these stray along the bark; at length resting upon the edge of a dark disc—a knot-hole in the tree. Into this her hand is plunged, and after a moment drawn out —empty!

At first there is no appearance of disappointment. On the contrary, the phosphoric gleam dimly lighting up her features, rather shows satisfaction—still further evinced in the phrase that falls from her lips, with the tone of its utterance. She says, contentedly :—

"*He has got it !*"

But by the same fitful light, soon after can be perceived a change—the slightest expression of chagrin, as she adds, in murmured interrogation,

"Why has he not left an answer ?"

Is she sure he has not ? No. But she soon will be.

With this determination, she again faces towards the tree; once more inserts her slender jewelled fingers; plunges in her white hand, to the wrist; gropes the cavity all round; then draws the hand out again, this time with an exclamation stronger than disappointment. The tone is of discontent—almost anger.

"He might at least have let me know whether he was coming or not—a word to say I might expect him. He should have been here before me ! I am certain it is the hour—past it !"

She is not so. It is but a conjecture; and in this she may be mistaken—perhaps wronging him. To make certain, she draws the watch from her waistbelt; steps out into the moonlight; and holds the dial close to her eyes. The gold glances bright, and the jewels flash joyfully under the moonbeams. But there is no joy in Helen Armstrong's face. On the contrary, a mixed expression of sadness and chagrin. For the hands of the watch point to ten minutes after the hour she had named in her letter.

There can be no mistake about the time—she had herself appointed it. And none in the time-piece. She has full confidence in her watch : it is not a cheap one.

"Ten minutes after, and he not here! No answer to my note! He must certainly have received it. Jule put it into the tree; she assured me of that on her return. Who but he could have taken it out? No one is likely to know of it. Oh! this is cruel! He comes not —I shall go home." ,

The cloak is once more closed around her; the hood drawn over her head.

Still she lingers—lingers and listens.

No footstep; no sound to break the stillness of the night; only the chirrup of tree-crickets, and the shrieking of owls.

She takes a last look at her watch—sadly, despairingly. It shows fifteen minutes after the appointed hour—nearer twenty! She restores it to its place, with an air of determination. Sadness, despair, chagrin—all three disappear from her countenance. Anger is now its expression, fixed and stern. The coruscation of the firefly has a response in flashes less pale than its own phosphorescence—sparks from the eyes of an indignant woman! Helen Armstrong is surely this; as, closely drawing her cloak around her, she turns away from the tree.

She has not passed beyond the shadow of its branches, ere her steps are stayed. A rustling of fallen leaves—a swishing among those that still adhere to their branches—a footfall with tread solid and heavy—the footfall of a man!

The figure of one is seen; indistinctly at first, but surely a man.

"He has been detained by some good cause," she joyfully reflects; her sadness and spite both departing, as he appears drawing nigh.

They are gone as he stands by her side.

But, womanlike, determined to make a grace of forgiveness, she begins by upbraiding him.

"You are here at last, sir! Well, I wonder you came at all. There's an old adage, 'Better lace than never.' Perhaps you think it fitting? Speaking of myself, you may be mistaken. Never mind! Whether or not, I've been here long enough, alone. And the hour is too late for me to stay any longer. So good night, sir— good night!"

Her speeches are spiteful in tone, and bitter in sense. She intends them to be both.

While giving utterance to them, she has drawn the hood over her head, and is moving off—as if determined to give a lesson to the lover who has slighted her.

Seeing this, he throws himself in front, interrupting her steps. Despite the darkness, she can perceive that his arms are in the air, and stretched towards her appealingly. The attitude speaks apology, regret, contrition—everything to make her relent.

She relents; is ready to fling herself, forgivingly, on his breast. But not without one more word of upbraiding.

" 'Tis cruel thus to have tried me. Oh ! Charles ! Charles ! why have you done so ?"

" Helen Armstrong, my name is not Charles, but Richard. *I am Richard Darke !*"

CHAPTER X.

THE WRONG MAN.

RICHARD DARKE instead of Charles Clancy!

Disappointment! This would be too tame a word to express the pang that shot through the heart of Helen Armstrong, on discovering the mistake she had made. It was bitter vexation, with a commingling of shame. For her words, though spoken in reproach, had terribly compromised her.

She did not sink to the earth, nor yet show signs of fainting. She was not a woman of this way. No cry came from her lips—nothing that could betray surprise, or even ordinary emotion.

As Darke stood before her with arms upraised, right in her path, she simply said :—

"Well, sir; if you *are* Richard Darke, what

then? Your being so does not give you any right to intrude upon me. I wish to be alone."

The cool, firm tone caused him to quail. He had hoped that the surprise of his unexpected appearance—coupled with his knowledge of her clandestine appointment — would have done something to subdue, perhaps make her submissive.

On the contrary, the thought of this last but stung her to resentment, and he soon saw it. His arms came down; and he was about stepping aside and leaving her free to pass; though not without making an attempt to justify himself. He did so, saying:—

"If I've intruded upon you, Miss Armstrong, I am sorry for it. It has been altogether an accident, I assure you. Having heard you were about to leave the neighbourhood—indeed, that you start to-morrow morning—I was going over to your father's house to say farewell. I am sorry that my coming this way, and chancing to meet you, should lay me open to the charge of intrusion. I shall still more regret, if it has interfered with an appointment. Some one else expected, I suppose ?"

For a time she was silent—abashed by the impudent interrogatory.

Recovering herself, she said :—

"And even so, what gives you the right to question me? I have told you I wish to be alone."

"Oh, if it's your wish, I shall at once relieve you of my presence."

He stepped to one side in saying so. Then continued—

"As I've said, I am on the way to your father's house to take leave of the family. If you are not going immediately home, perhaps I may be the bearer of a message for you ?"

The irony was evident; but Helen Armstrong was not thinking of this. Only how she could get disembarrassed of this man who had appeared at a moment so *mal-apropos*. Charles Clancy—for he was the expected one—might have been detained by some cause unknown, a delay still possible of justification. She had a lingering hope he might yet come, and her eye interrogated the forest with a quick, subtle glance.

Notwithstanding its subtlety, notwithstanding the obscurity surrounding them, Darke saw it—understood it.

Without waiting for a rejoinder, he proceeded to say—

"From the mistake you have just made, Miss Armstrong, I presume you took me for some one bearing the baptismal name of Charles. In these parts I know only one person who carries that cognomen—Charles Clancy. If it be he you are expecting, I think I can save you the necessity of staying out in the night air any longer; that is, if you are staying for him. He will certainly not come."

"What mean you, Mr. Darke? Why do you say that?"

The disappointing speech had made its impression, and thrown the proud girl off her guard. She spoke confusedly, and without reflection.

Darke's rejoinder was more cunning: a studied one.

"Because I met Charles Clancy this morning, and he told me he was going off on a journey. He was just starting when I saw him. Some affair of the heart, I believe; a little love-scrape he's got into with a pretty Creole who lives in Natchez. By-the-way, he showed me a photograph of yourself, which he said he had just received. A very excellent likeness, I call it. Excuse me for telling you, that Clancy and I came near quarrelling about that picture. He had another photograph, that of his Creole *chère-amie*, and would insist that she is more beautiful than you. It is true, Miss Armstrong, that you've given me no great reason for being your champion. Still, I couldn't stand that; and, after questioning Clancy's taste, I plainly told him he was mistaken. I'm ready to repeat the same to him, or anyone who says you are not the most beautiful woman in the State of Mississippi."

At the conclusion of the fulsome speech Helen Armstrong cared but little for his championship, and not much for anything else.

Her heart was nigh to breaking. She had

given her affections to Charles Clancy—in her letter late written had lavished them.

And they had been trifled with—scorned. She was slighted for a Creole girl! There was full proof, or how could Darke have known of it? More maddening still, Clancy had been making boast of her suppliance and shame, showing her photograph, and proclaiming the triumph he had obtained! O God!

This was the ejaculation that escaped from Helen Armstrong's lips, as the bitter thoughts swept through her soul. Along with it came a half-suppressed scream, as, despairingly, she turned her face homeward.

Darke saw his opportunity, or thought so; and again flung himself before her.

"Helen Armstrong!" he cried, in the earnestness of passion—a passion, if not pure, at least heartfelt and strong—"why should you care for a man who thus mocks you? Here am I, who love you truly—madly—more than my own life! It's not too late to withdraw the answer you have given me. Gainsay it now, and there will

be no need for any change—any going to Texas.
Your father's home may still be his, and yours.
Say you will be my wife, and everything shall be
restored to him—all will be well."

She listened for the conclusion of the speech.
Its appealing sincerity stayed her, though she
could not tell, or did not think, why. It was a
moment of mechanical irresolution.

But, soon as it was ended, again came back
into her soul the bitterness that had just swept
through it.

And there was no balm in the words spoken
by Richard Darke; on the contrary, his speech
was like pouring in fresh poison.

To his appeal she made answer, as once before
she had answered him—with but a single word.
It was repeated three times, and in a tone not to
be mistaken. On speaking it, she parted from
the spot; her proud, haughty step, with a denying if not disdainful gesture, telling him, she was
not to be further accosted.

Spited, chagrined, angry as he was, in his
craven heart he felt cowed and fearful. He dared

not follow her, but remained under the tree, from whose hollow trunk still seemed to reverberate her last word, thrice emphatically pronounced—

" *Never—never—never !* "

CHAPTER XI.

"WHY COMES HE NOT?"

IF, on that night, Helen Armstrong went to bed reflecting bitterly of Charles Clancy, there was another woman, who sat up, thinking sadly about him.

Some two miles from the gate of Colonel Armstrong's plantation, near the road that led past the latter, stood a house, of humble aspect compared with the dwelling of the planter. It might have been called a cottage; but the name is scarcely known in the State of Mississippi. Nor yet was it either log-cabin, or "shanty;" but a frame-house, with walls of "weather boarding," planed and painted, the roof being of "shingles." It was a class of dwelling occasionally seen in the Southern States—though not so frequently as in the Northern—inhabited by men in moderate circumstances, poorer than planters, but richer or more gentle than the "white trash," who live in log-cabins.

Planters they are in social rank, though poor; perhaps owning three or four slaves, and cultivating a small holding of land, from twenty to fifty acres. A frame-house vouches for their respectability, while two or three log structures at the back, representing barn, stable, and other outbuildings, tell of there being land attached.

Of this class was the habitation spoken of as standing two miles from the gate of the Armstrong plantation. It was the home of Charles Clancy; and inside it was the woman whose thoughts about him on that night we have described as being sad. He was her son—her only child, and she his only living parent.

As already known, her widowhood was of recent date. She still wore its emblems upon her person, and carried its sorrow in her heart.

Her husband, of good Irish lineage, had found his way to Nashville, the capital city of

Tennessee; where, in times long past, many Irish families had made settlement. It was there he had married her, she herself being a native Tennessean, sprung from the old Carolina pioneer stock, that had gone into the country near the end of the eighteenth century, along with the Robertsons, Hyneses, Hardings, and Bradfords, leaving to their descendants a certain patent of nobility, or at least a family name deserving, and generally obtaining, respect.

In America, as elsewhere, it is not the rule for Irishmen to grow rich; and still more exceptional in the case of an Irish gentleman. When these have riches their hospitality is too apt to take the shape of a spendthrift profuseness, ending in pecuniary embarrassment.

It was so with Captain Jack Clancy, who got wealth with his wife, but soon squandered it upon his own and his wife's friends. The result was a move to Mississippi, where land was at the time cheaper, and where his attenuated fortune enabled him to hold out a little longer.

Still the property he had purchased in Missis-

sippi State was but a poor one ; and he was contemplating a further flit into the rich "red lands"
of North Eastern Texas, then becoming famous
as a field for colonisation. As said, his son
Charles had been sent thither on a trip of
exploration; spent twelve months upon the
frontier prospecting for their new home ; and returned with a report in every way favourable.

But the ear into which it was to have been
spoken could no more hear. Before his return,
Captain Clancy was in his coffin; and to the only
son there remained only a mother.

This was several weeks antecedent to the
tragedy, whose details are already before the
reader. Charles had passed the intervening time
in endeavouring to console his dearly-beloved
mother, whose grief, pressing heavily, had almost
brought her to the grave. It was one of a long
series of reverses which had sorely taxed her
fortitude. Another of the like, and the tomb
might close over her.

Some such presentiment was in her mind, on
that very day as the sun went down, and she

sate beside a dim candle, her ear keenly bent to listen for the returning footsteps of her son.

He had been absent since noon. He had gone out deer-stalking, so he had told her. She could spare him for this, and pardon a prolonged absence. She knew he was devoted to the chase; he had been so from a boy; but more than ever since his trip to Texas, where he had imbibed a passion for it—or, rather, cultivated, that instinctive to him. While in Texas he had made an expedition to the farthest frontier, and there hunted buffalo and grizzly bear, with trappers and Indians for his companions. Thus inoculated, a man rarely gets over his penchant for the pursuit sanctified by St. Hubert. His mother, knowing this, would have thought nothing of his staying out a little late.

But on the present occasion he was beyond the usual time. It was now night; the deer must have sought their coverts; and he had not gone " torch-hunting."

Only one thing could she think of that might explain the tardiness of his return. The eyes of

the mother had been of late watchful and wary.
She had noticed her son's abstracted air, and
heard sighs that seemed to come from his inner
heart. Who could mistake the signs of love,
either in man or woman? Mrs. Clancy could
not, and did not. She saw that her son had
fallen into this condition.

Rumours that seemed wafted on the air—signs
slight, but significant—perhaps the whisper of a
confidential servant—these had given her assurance of the fact: telling her, at the same time,
who had won his affections—Helen Armstrong.

The mother was not displeased. In all the
neighbourhood there was no woman she would
have more wished for her daughter-in-law than
this young lady. Not from any thought of her
remarkable beauty, or high social standing.
Caroline Clancy was herself too well descended
to make much of the latter circumstance. It was
the reputed noble character of the lady that
influenced her approval of her son's choice.

Thinking of this—remembering her own youth
and the stolen interviews with Charles Clancy's

father—often under the shadows of night—she could not reflect harshly on the absence of that father's son from his home, however late the hour.

It was only when the clock struck twelve, she began to think seriously about it. Then came over her a feeling of uneasiness, soon changing to apprehension. Why should he be staying out so late—after midnight? The same little bird, that brought her tidings of her son's love affair, had also told her it was clandestine. Mrs. Clancy might not have liked this. It had the semblance of a slight to them, the Clancys, in their reduced circumstances. But then, to satisfy her, came up the retrospect of her own days of courtship.

Still, at that hour the young lady could not—dared not—be abroad. All the more unlikely that the Armstrongs were going away—as all the neighbourhood knew—and intended starting early the next morning.

Colonel Armstrong's household would long since have retired to rest; and an interview with his daughter could not be the cause of

Charles Clancy's detention. Something else must be keeping him. What?

Thus ran the reflections of the fond mother. At intervals she started from her seat, as some sound reached her from without; each time gliding to the door and looking out—only to return to her room disappointed.

For long spells she stood in the porch, her eye interrogating the road that ran past the cottage, her ear keenly listening for footsteps.

There was a brilliant moonlight. But no man, no form moving underneath it. No sound of coming feet—only dead stillness, saving the nocturnal voices of the forest—the chirp of tree-crickets, the gluck-gluck of frogs, and the shrieking of owls. But among them no sound bearing resemblance to a footfall.

One o'clock, and still silence, or the same mono-tone of animal sounds; to the mother of Charles Clancy now become terribly oppressive, as with keen apprehension she watched for his return.

At short intervals she glanced at the little "Connecticut" clock that ticked over the mantel.

A pedlar's thing, it might be false, as the men who came south selling them. It was the reflection of a southern woman, and she hoped her conjecture might be true.

But, as she lingered in the porch, and looked at the waning moon, she knew it must be late—quite two o'clock. And still no fall of footsteps—no son returning.

"Where, where, is my Charles? What can be detaining him?"

Phrases almost identical with those that had fallen from the lips of Helen Armstrong but a few hours before! The place only unlike, and the words prompted by a different passion, though one equally strong and pure.

Both doomed to disappointment alike hard to bear. Alike in cause, and yet how dissimilar the impression produced! The sweetheart believing herself slighted, forsaken, left without a lover; the mother tortured with the presentiment she no longer had a son!

When, at an hour between midnight and morning, a dog, his coat clotted with mud, came crawl-

ing through the gate, and Mrs. Clancy recognised
her son's favourite hunting hound, she could still
only have suspicion of the terrible truth. But
it was a suspicion that, to the mother's heart,
already filled with foreboding, felt like certainty. Too much for her strength. Wearied
and worn with watching, prostrated by the in-
tensity of her vigil, when the hound crawled up
the steps of the porch and under the dim light
she saw his bedraggled form—blood as well as
mud upon it—the sight produced a climax, a
shock nearly fatal.

Mrs. Clancy swooned upon the spot, and was
carried inside the house by a faithful negro slave
—the last that was left to her.

CHAPTER XII.

A LAST LOOK AT LOVED SCENES.

LONG before the hour of daybreak on that same morning, a light waggon, loaded with luggage and other personal effects, passed out from the gate of what had lately been Archibald Armstrong's plantation.

It was his no more. The mortgage had been foreclosed, and Ephraim Darke was now its owner.

Close following the baggage waggon was a carriage of lighter construction, the old family barouche, inside which were seated Colonel Armstrong and his two daughters. They were all of family he had; and it was the last time they were ever to ride in that carriage, either for airing or journey.

It was a journey on which they were now

bent; not a very long one by carriage—only to Natchez; whence a steam-boat would convey them, along with other passengers, up the Red River of Louisiana.

The boat was not to start before daybreak; but there were some miles, and much rough road, between the plantation and the town of Natchez; hence the early hour of removal from a house never more to be their home.

Colonel Armstrong had chosen the boat, as the time of departure, for a special reason. Feeling himself a bankrupt, broken man, he did not desire to be seen leaving his old home under the glaring light of day. Not that he had any fear of being detained. He had satisfied all legal claims, and had still something left—enough to give him a handsome start in Texas. He had converted it into cash; which will account for the accompaniment of only a single waggon, loaded with personal effects, and some endeared objects— such as compose the household gods of every old family. Half-a-dozen male and female slaves— Jule among the latter—were part of the retained chattels. His early start was due to a feeling of sensitiveness, not shame. He shrank from being stared at in his hour of humiliation.

By the light of a southern moon, the two vehicles, transporting him and his, rumbled along the road, or sank into its ruts; at length, entering the quaint old city of Natchez; which stands upon one of those very rare projections that surmount the Mississippi river, known as the " Chicasaw Bluffs."

It was still not quite day when he and his belongings, after slowly crawling down the steep hill that leads to the river landing, got aboard the boat; and only just sunrise as the steamer's bell, tolling for the third time, proclaimed the signal of departure.

Soon after, Colonel Armstrong and his two daughters, standing upon the "guards" outside the ladies' cabin, looked their last on the city of Natchez; in the best society of which they had for many years mingled, and where the eldest had reigned supreme. It was no thought of parting from this pleasant ascendancy — no thought of exchanging her late luxurious life for the log cabin and poverty her father had promised her—that brought the tear into Helen Armstrong's eye. She could have borne all these, and far more—ay, looked forward to them with cheerfulness—had Charles Clancy been true.

He had not, and that was an end of it.

Was it ?

No; not for her, though it might be for him. In the company of his new sweetheart, the Creole girl of whom Dick Darke had given her the first information — for Helen Armstrong had never heard of her before—he would soon forget the vows he had made, and the sweet words spoken under the magnolia; a tree that, in retrospect, seemed now to her sadder than any cypress.

Would she ever forget him ? Could she ? No, not unless in Texas, whither she was going, there should be found the fabled Lethean stream. She thought not of this. If she had, it would not have been with faith in the efficacy of its waters. There was no water on earth, nor spirit, that

could give either oblivion, or solace, to the
thoughts that tortured her.

Perhaps not less sad, though very different,
would they have been if she had but known the
truth.   If, instead of making that early start
from the old plantation home, her father had
waited for daybreak, all would have been different—all that affected her happiness.   Had the
carriage conveying Colonel Armstrong and his
daughters but rolled along the road when the
sun was shining upon it, they would have heard
tidings—a tale to thrill all three, but more
especially herself.   With her it would have penetrated to the heart's inmost core, displacing the
bitterness there already lodged by one also
galling, though unlike in nature.   Perhaps it
might have been easier to endure ?   Perhaps
Helen Armstrong would rather have believed
Charles Clancy dead, than think of his traitorous
defection ?

: Which of the two calamities she would have
preferred—preferring neither—there could be no
opportunity of testing.   Long before it was

known that Clancy had been killed—before the hue-and-cry was raised, resounding through the settlement—the boat on which the Armstrongs were embarked had steamed far away from the scene of the tragedy.

Little thought Helen, as she stood on the stern-guard, looking back with tearful eyes, that the man making her weep was at that moment a corpse, lying cold under shadowy cypresses.

Had she known it, she would have been shedding tears—not of spite, but sorrow.

CHAPTER XIII.

WHAT HAS BECOME OF THE CORPSE?

THE sun was up—high up over the tops of the tallest forest trees. Around the residence of the widow Clancy a crowd had collected. They were mostly men, with an admixture of boys, half-grown youths, and women. They were her nearest neighbours; while those who dwelt at a greater distance were still in the act of assembling. Every few minutes two or three horsemen were seen riding up, carrying long rifles over their shoulders, with powder-horns and bullet-pouches strapped across their breasts. Those already upon the ground were similarly armed and ac-coutred.

The cause of this warlike muster was known to all. That morning at an early hour, a report had been spread throughout the plantations, that Charles Clancy was missing from his home, under circumstances that justified a suspicion of foul play having befallen him. His mother had sent messengers to and fro; and this had brought the gathering around her house.

In the South-Western States, on occasions of this kind, it does not do for anyone to show indifference, whatever be his station in life. The proudest or wealthiest planter, as well as the poorest white, is expected to take part in the administration of backwoods justice—sometimes not strictly *en règle* with the laws of the land.

For this reason every neighbour, far and near, summoned or not summoned, is pretty sure to be present; as they were on this occasion. Among the rest Ephraim Darke and his son Richard.

When all, or nearly all, had got upon the ground, the business that brought them together was discussed. It was to search for Charles Clancy, still absent from his home. The mother's story had been already told, and only the late comers had to hear it again. Her son had gone

out deer-hunting, as often, almost every day,
before. He had taken his favourite hound with
him. She knew not in what direction he had
gone. It had never been her habit to inquire
which way he went on his hunting expeditions.
Enough for her that he came home again; which,
until that day, he had always done before the
going down of the sun. He had never before
stayed out after night. He knew she was alone;
and, being a good son, always returned within
the twilight, if not sooner. Having failed to do
so on the night before, she naturally felt uneasy.
At a later hour her uneasiness became alarm.
Later still, she was in a state of agonized apprehension; which came to its climax when, in the
grey light of morning, the dog came skulking
home, his coat covered with mud, and blood
upon it.

The animal was before their eyes, still in the
condition spoken of. They could all see it had
been shot — the tear of a bullet was visible
upon its neck, having cut through the skin. Besides, there was a piece of cord knotted around

the dog's throat, the other end showing as if it had been first gnawed by the animal's teeth, and then broken off as with a pluck.

All these circumstances had a significance; though no one could explain or even offer a conjecture as to their meaning. It looked as if the animal had been tied—perhaps to a tree—and afterwards succeeded in setting itself loose.

But why tied? And why had it been shot? These were the questions that not anybody could answer.

Strange, too, in the hound having reached home at the hour it did! Its missing master was never abroad after sunset—so Mrs. Clancy assured them. If anything had happened to him before that hour—anything to separate him from the dog and keep him back—why had the latter delayed returning home? As Clancy had gone out about the middle of the day, he could not have proceeded to such a distance from the house for his hound to have been nearly all night in getting back to it.

Was it he himself who fired the bullet whose

mark was made upon the dog? This was also a point in the preliminary investigation.

Not for long. The question was soon answered. There were old backwoodsmen among the mustered crowd—hunters who knew how to interpret a "sign" as exactly as would Champollion an Egyptian hieroglyph. These having examined the score on the hound's skin, pronounced the bullet to have come from a *smooth-bore, and not a rifle.* It was known that Charles Clancy never hunted with a smooth-bore, but always with a rifle.

This was a point of very important character, and did not fail to make impression on the minds of the assembled backwoodsmen.

After some time spent in discussing what was best to be done, it was at length agreed to institute a search for the missing man. In the presence of his mother no one spoke of searching for his *body;* though there was a general apprehension that this would be the end of it.

She, most interested of all, had a too true foreboding of it. When her neighbours, starting out, told her to be of good cheer, her heart more truly said to her, she would never see her son again.

On leaving the house the searchers separated into three distinct parties, intending to take different directions; which they did.

With one of these, and the largest, went the dog; an old hunter, named Simeon Woodley, conducting it. It was thought that the animal might be in some way useful, if taken back on his tracks—supposing that these could be discovered. Along with this party went Richard Darke, his father choosing to accompany another.

Just as had been conjectured, the dog did prove useful. Once inside the woods, without even setting snout to the ground, he started off upon a straight run—going so swiftly that it was difficult for the horsemen to keep up with him.

It put them all into a gallop; continued for two miles through woodland, to the edge of the swamp. Here it ended, by their all pulling up under a tree—a great buttressed cypress, by the side of which the staghound had made stop, and commenced a lugubrious baying.

The searchers, having ridden up, dismounted, and gathered around the spot; many of them expecting to see the dead body of Charles Clancy.

But there was no body there—dead or alive. Only a large pile of Spanish moss, that appeared to have been recently torn from the branches above. It looked as though it had been first collected into a heap, and then scattered apart.

The dog had taken stand in a central spot, from which the parasite had been disturbed, and there stood, giving tongue. As the men drew closer and bent their eyes upon the ground, they saw something red upon it; which proved to be blood. It was dark crimson, almost black, and coagulated. Still, was it blood.

From under the edge of the moss-heap protruded the barrel of a gun. On kicking the loose cover aside, they saw it was a rifle —of the kind common among backwoodsmen. There were many present who identified the piece, as that which belonged to Charles Clancy.

More of the moss being removed, a hat was discovered. It was Clancy's! Half a score of the searchers knew the hat — could swear to it.

During all this time Richard Darke remained in the background, not taking an active part in the scrutiny. This was strange, too. Up to that moment he had been, to all appearance, amongst the foremost and most zealous.

Why did he now hold back? Why stand with pallor upon his cheeks, eyes sunken in their sockets, teeth chattering, as if an ague chill had suddenly attacked him?

It would have been fortunate for him had no one taken notice of his reticence and changed appearance. But some one had. Simeon Woodley had, and others as well. Despite the obscure light under the shadow of the cypress, Darke's strange behaviour and scared looks were observed.

Something besides—something yet more signilicant — attracted the attention of his fellow-searchers. Once or twice, as he approached the blood-stained spot, the dog sprang towards him with a fierce growl, and continued it until beaten off!

Men made note of the matter, but no comments at the time. They were too much occupied with conjectures as to what had actually occurred. Death to Charles Clancy they were now convinced; and proceeded with the search for his body.

All around, the forest was explored; along the swamp edge: up and down the sides of the sluggish creek that ran close by.

Several hours were spent by them in tramping about. But not a trace could be found of living man, or dead body. The searchers only looked for the last. Not one of them had the slightest hope of Clancy being still alive. How could they, with such evidence of his death before their eyes?

Nor was there any doubt about his having been killed. There was no sign to make them think he had shot himself, or otherwise committed suicide. All they had yet seen, or heard, or knew, pointed to assassination — to stark, downright murder.

But what had become of the corpse? If carried away, why? Who could have carried it away? Wherefore and whither? And for what reason surreptitiously? An accumulation of mysteries!

Puzzled, almost awed by them, the searchers at length left the ground. Not, however, until after giving it that sort of investigation that satisfies the instincts of a crowd. They had spent most part of the day in this, without thinking of aught else, not even of their dinners. But night was approaching: they had grown hungry; and one after another hurried towards their homes; at first in odd individuals, then in straggling groups; the movement at length becoming general. They went home, determined to return on the following day, and, if necessary, renew the search.

Only two men stayed—Simeon Woodley and

a companion, a young backwoodsman—like himself, a professional hunter.

"I'm darned glad they're gone off," said Woodley, as soon as the two were left alone. "Dan Boone himself kedn't take up a track wi' sech a noisy clanjamfrey aroun' him. I've tuk notice o' somethin', Ned, the which I didn't weesh to make known whiles they war about—'specially while Dick Darke war on the groun'. Le's go now, and see if thar's anythin' to be made out o' it."

The young hunter, whose name was Heywood —Edward Heywood—simply made sign of assent, and followed his elder *confrère.*

After walking about two hundred yards through the forest, Woodley made stop beside a cypress "knee," with his face towards it, and his eyes fixed upon a spot nearly on a level with his chin. It was one of the largest of these singular vegetable excrescences that perplex the botanist.

"You see that, Ned?" said the old hunter, at the same time extending his finger to point out something near the summit of the "knee."

The last Heywood did not need. His eyes were already on the object.

" I see a bullet-hole, sure—-and something red around the edge of it. Looks like blood ?"

" It *air* blood, an' nothin' else. It's a bullet-hole, too; and the bit o' lead lodged in thar has fust passed through some critter's skin. Else why shed thar a been blood on it ? Let's dig it out, and see what we kin make o' it."

Woodley took a knife from his pocket; and, springing open the blade, inserted it into the bark of the cypress, close to the bullet-hole. He did this dexterously and with caution; taking care not to touch the encrimsoned orifice the ball had made, or in any way alter its appearance. Making a circular incision around, and gradually deepening it, he at length extracted the bit of lead, along with the wood in which it had got imbedded. He knew there was a gun-bullet inside. The point of his knife-blade told him so. He had probed the hole, before commencing to cut it out.

Weighing the piece of wood in his hand, and

then passing it into that of his companion, he said—

" Ned, this here chunk o' timmer's got a bullet inside o' it that nivir kim out o' any rifle. Thar's big eends o' an ounce weight o' it. Only a smooth-bore ked a discharged sech."

" You're right there," answered Heywood, in like manner testing the ponderosity of the piece. " It's the ball of a smooth-bore, no doubt of it."

"Well, then, who carries a smooth-bore through these hyar woods ?   Who, Ned Heywood ?"

" I know only one man who does."

" Name him !   Name the d——d rascal !"

" Dick Darke."

" Ye may drink afore me, Ned.   That's the skunk I war a-thinkin' 'bout, an' hev been all the day.   I seed other sign beside this—the which escaped the eyes o' the rest.   An' I'm gled it did : for I didn't want Dick Darke to be about when I war follerin' it up.   For that reezun I drawed the people aside—so as none o' em shed notice it. By good luck they didn't."

" What other sign have you seen ?"

" Tracks in the mud, clost in by the edge o' the swamp. They're a good bit from the place whar the poor young fellur hez gone down, an' makin' away from it. I got only a glimp at 'em, but ked see they'd been made by a man runnin'. You bet yur life on't they war made by a pair o' boots I've see Dick Darke wearin'. It's too gloomsome now to make anythin' out o' em. So let's you an' me go by ourselves in the mornin' at the earliest o' daybreak, afore the people git about. Then we kin gie them tracks a thorrer scrutination. If they don't prove to be Dick Darke's, then call Sime Woodley a thick-headed woodchuck."

" How shall we know them to be his ? If we only had his boots, so that we might compare them ?"

" *If!* Thar's no if. We *shall* hev his boots— boun' to hev 'em."

" But how are we to get them ?"

" Leave that to me. I've thought o' a plan to git purssession o' the skunk's futwear, an' every- thin' else belongin' to him that kin throw light

on this dark bizness. Come, Ned! Le's go now
to the widder's house, an' see if we ken say a
word o' comfort to the poor lady—for a lady she
air.   Belike enough this thing'll be the death
o' her. She warn't strong at best, an' she's been
a deal weaker since the husban' died. Now the
son's goed too. Come on, Heywood! Le's show
her she ain't forsook by everybody."

"I'm with you, Woodley!"

CHAPTER XIV.

THE SLEEP OF THE ASSASSIN.

THE night after Clancy's assassination Richard Darke did not sleep soundly. He scarce slept at all. Two causes kept him awake—the weight of guilt upon his soul, and the sting of scornful words yet ringing in his ear—these last uttered by the woman he loved—wildly worshipped.

Either should have been sufficient to torture him, and did—the last more than the first. He had no remorse for having killed the man, but much chagrin at having been slighted by the woman. The slight had contributed to the crime, making the latter less repented of. Had it served his purpose, there would have been no thought of repentance. But it had not. He had done murder, and made nothing out of it. For this reason only did he regret having done it.

In his half waking, half dreaming, slumbers, he fancied he could hear the howling of a hound. It awoke him; but when awake, he thought no more of it, or only with a transient apprehension. His thoughts were of Helen Armstrong—of her scorn, and his discomfiture. This was a sure thing now; and he could no longer hope. Next morning she would be gone from him—for ever. A steam-boat, leaving Natchez at the earliest hour of day, would convey Colonel Armstrong, with all his belongings, far away from the place. It would know them no more; and he, Richard Darke, in all probability would never again set eyes on the woman he loved—so madly as to have committed murder for her sake.

"Why the devil did I do it?"

In this coarse shape did he express himself, as he lay upon his couch—lightly thinking of the dread deed, but weightily grieving how little it had availed him.

Such were his reflections cn the first night

after it.   Far different were they on the second. Then Helen Armstrong was no more in his thoughts, or having there only a secondary place. Then the howls of the hound were heard, or fancied, more frequently.   They did not startle him from his sleep, for he slept not at all.   All night long he lay thinking of his crime, or rather of the peril in which it had placed him.

The events of the day had given him a clearer comprehension of things; and he now knew he was in danger.   No one had said anything to himself about the suspicion directed upon him.   Still there was the circumstance, which *might* be known, that he and Clancy were rival aspirants to the hand of Helen Armstrong.   He did not think it was known—he hoped not, as their rivalry would point to a motive for the murder. For all, he feared it.

He reviewed his own conduct throughout the day.   During the search, and in the presence of the searchers, he had borne himself satisfactorily. He had taken an active part, counterfeiting surprise, zeal, and sorrow equal to that felt by any

of the party, if not greater. It was the worst
thing he could have done: since it had attracted
observation. Though he had not noticed it, eyes
were upon him, keenly watching his every movement, and ears .listening to every speech he
uttered. There had been no change in his countenance that was not noted; and comments made
upon it—behind his back. As he had not heard
them, he then felt secure—though far from being
confidently so. He was only confident that there
was no evidence, except what might be called
circumstantial; and this only slight. For all, he
had at times, during the day, come very near convulsive trembling. Not from any remorse of conscience, but a cold shiver that crept over him as
he approached the spot where the deed had been
done. And when he at length stood upon it,
under the sombre shadow of the cypress, among
the moss with which he had shrouded the corpse;
when he saw that it was no longer there, his
fear was intensified. It became awe—dread,
mysterious awe. Sure of having there left a
dead body—the only one sure of this—what had

become of it? Had the dead come to life again? Had Charles Clancy, shot through the breast—he had noted the place, by the blood gushing from it, as he held the picture before his victim's face— could Clancy have again risen to his feet? Could a man, having his body bored by a three-quarter-ounce ball, and laid prostrate along the earth, ever get up again? Was it possible for him to have survived?

As the murderer put these questions to himself, on the spot where the murder had been committed, no wonder he was awed, as well as mystified—no wonder his features showed that singular expression—so peculiar as to have attracted attention! They who noticed it, however, said nothing —at least, in his presence.

The dog had not been so reticent. As we have said, the dumb brute seemed also to have taken note of his weird, wild look, and had repeatedly barked at him.

Darke had preserved sufficient presence of mind to explain this to the searching party; telling them he had once corrected the hound while out hunting with *his friend* Clancy, and that ever since the animal had shown hostility to him!

The tale was plausible. For all this, it did not deceive those to whom he told it. Some of them drew deductions from it, still more unfavourable to the teller.

But if the mystery of the missing body had troubled him during the day—in the hour when his blood was up, and his nerves strung with ex-citement—in the night, in the dark silent hours, as he lay tossing upon his couch, it more than troubled, more than awed—it horrified him.

In vain he tried to compose himself, by shaping an explanation of the mystery. He could not comprehend it; he could not even form a pro-bable conjecture. Was Clancy dead, or still living? Had he walked away from the ground? Or been carried from it, a corpse?

In either case the danger to him, Darke, would be almost equal. Better, of course, if Clancy were dead. For then there would be but cir-cumstantial evidence against his assassin. If alive, he could himself give testimony of the attempt; which criminally would be almost the same.

Darke hoped he was dead. The night before he felt sure of it. Not so now. As he lay tossing on his couch—struggling with distracted thoughts — with fears that appalled him — he would have given the best runaway nigger he had ever caught, to be assured of Charles Clancy being a corpse.

And he would have granted to half a score of his father's slaves their full freedom—cheerfully given it—if this could have guaranteed him against detection, or punishment.

He was being punished, if not through remorse of conscience, by craven fear. He now knew how hard it is to sleep the sleep of the assassin, or lie awake upon a murderer's bed.

CHAPTER XV.

To the mother of Charles Clancy it was a day of dread suspense while they were abroad searching for her son. Far more fearful the night after they had returned—not without tidings of the missing man. Such tidings! The too certain assurance of his death—of his having been assassinated, with no trace of the assassin, and no clue to the whereabouts of the body.

The mother's grief, hitherto kept in check by a still lingering hope, now escaped all bounds, and became truly agonising. Her heart seemed broken; if not, surely was it breaking.

Although, in her poverty without many friends, she was not left alone in her sorrow. It could not be so in the far South-west. Several of her neighbours—rough backwoodsmen though they were—having kind hearts under their coarse homespun coats, determined to stay with her through the night.

They remained outside in the porch, smoking their pipes, conversing of the occurrences of the day, and the mystery of the murder.

At first they spoke cautiously, two and two, and only in whispers. These gradually became mutterings pronounced in louder tone; while the name of Richard Darke was frequently mentioned. He was not among the men remaining in the widow Clancy's cottage.

Soon the conversation grew general; those who took part in it expressing themselves more openly, until, at length, Dick Darke—as, for short, his neighbours called him—became the sole topic of discourse.

His behaviour during the day had not escaped their notice. Even the most stolid among them had remarked a strangeness in it. In his counterfeited zeal he had overdone himself. The sharpest of the searchers only observed this; but all were

more or less struck with something beyond surprise, when they saw the dog turn upon and
bark at him. What could that mean ?

Just as one had put this interrogatory, and
answers or surmises were being offered, the same
dog—the hound—was heard again giving tongue.
The animal had sprung out from the porch and
commenced barking, as if some person was
making approach to the house. Almost simultaneously the little wicket gate in front turned
on its hinges.

A negro, the only one attached to the establishment, quieted the dog ; went out, and spoke to
the party at the gate. Only a few muttered
words were exchanged. Then the negro came
back to the house—two men following close
upon his heels. These were Simeon Woodley
and Ned Heywood.

The others, recognising, rose to receive them;
and the new comers became part of the conclave,
still discussing the events of the day.

Woodley, looked up to by all, as the man most
likely to throw light on the series of mysteries

perplexing them, soon became chief speaker—the rest hearkening to him as if he were an oracle.

There was no loud talking done. On the contrary, the discussion was carried on in a low tone —at times almost in whispers—the little group permitted to take part in it keeping their heads close together, so that the women and others should not hear what was said.

They who thus deliberated were in darkness. At least there was no light in the porch where they sat, except what came from the occasional flash of a candle, carried across the corridor from room to room. When this flitted over their faces, it showed upon one and all of them, an expression different from that likely to be called forth by any ordinary conversation. Eyes could be seen sparkling with passion—as of anger, held in restraint; lips tightly pressed upon teeth that seemed set determinedly on some purpose, wanting only an additional word to give it the cue for action.

The same candle's gleam revealed the form of Simeon Woodley in the centre of the group, holding in his hand an object which, without being told what it was, no one could have recognised. But they to whom he was exhibiting it knew well. It was a piece of cypress wood, inside of which was the bullet of a gun. They had received full explanations as to how the ball had been thus buried, and saw the blood tinge around the orifice it had made on entering. In short, they had been made aware of everything already known to the two hunters.

Other circumstances were stated and discussed; and to a select few Woodley communicated his discovery of the footprints, as also his conjecture about the boots that might be found to correspond to them.

How he was to confirm this to himself, and prove it to the others, was also made known to this same select few; who, shortly after, mounting their horses, rode away from the house, leaving enough friends to stay by the afflicted woman—to give her their company, if they could not comfort her in her affliction.

The men who rode off with Woodley, instead

of scattering, each to his own home, kept together along the road leading to the county town. When near its suburb, they stopped at a large house— known to be the residence of the sheriff.

A knock at the door, a summons to this official, and he was soon in their midst. A word or two from Woodley; and, hastily ordering his horse, he mounted and placed himself at their head.

Then all turned back along the road, as if going again to the house of Mrs. Clancy.

Not so, however. Instead, the cavalcade at a crossing took a different direction, and headed towards the plantation of Ephraim Darke; the gate of which they passed through, just as dawn began to dapple the eastern sky.

Before daylight had declared itself, they halted in front of the house; half a dozen men detaching themselves from the main body, and riding round to its rear, as if to guard against the escape of the inmates.

He, the cause of these precautionary movements, was still abed; tossing, as throughout all the night, upon a sleepless couch. But his midnight

agony was easy, compared with that he was called
upon to endure, when the morning light came
through the window of his chamber, and along
with it voices.   They were many and strange, all
speaking in tones of vengeance.

The assassin sprang to his feet, and, rushing
across the room, looked out. It did not need
this to tell him what the noise was about. His
guilty heart had already guessed it. Among
the half-score horsemen who had drawn up
around the house, he recognised the sheriff of
the county, and beside him two others, whom he
knew to be Woodley and Heywood.

These three had already dismounted, and were
entering the door.

In ten seconds after, they were inside his sleep-
ing-chamber; the sheriff, as he stepped across its
threshold, saying, in a firm, clear voice,

"Richard Darke, I arrest you !"

"For what ?"

"*For the murder of Charles Clancy !*"

CHAPTER XVI.

A SOUTH-WESTERN SHERIFF.

AFTER his arrest, Richard Darke was to be conveyed to the county gaol—about three miles from his father's residence.

The men, who had made him prisoner, took note of every circumstance attending the arrest They searched the chamber in which he had slept—the whole house, in fact. There were few of them who owed Ephraim Darke any goodwill, but many the contrary. His accumulated wealth, used only for selfish ends, had not gained him popularity in the neighbourhood. Besides, he was not a Southerner *pur sang,* as most of his neighbours were. They knew him to be from the New England States; and, although there was not a bit of Abolitionist in him, but much of the opposite, still he was not liked either by planter or "poor white."

The sheriff and his party, therefore, used little ceremony while in the act of making the arrest: ransacking the house, and examining its most sacred *arcana.* They took possession of the double-barrelled gun, which Richard was in the habit of carrying, as also the suit of clothes he usually wore when out in the woods. In the coat—it was noted this was not the same he had on during the day of the search—was found a hole that looked as if freshly made, and by a bullet! It was through the skirt, and had a torn, tattered edge.

Among the men present when he was made prisoner, were several who could read such sign, and interpret it as surely, or more surely, than an expert would identify a particular handwriting. Notably of these was the hunter Woodley. At a glance, he pronounced the hole in the coat-skirt to have been made by a bullet, and one that had passed through the barrel of a rifled gun.

Several others, after looking at it, confirmed Woodley's assertion.

The circumstance was significant; and led to renewed conjectures among those surrounding the sheriff.

No one thought of questioning the prisoner about it—not now, that he was in the hands of the law. All further formal investigation would be postponed till the trial, soon to take place. The party arresting him only busied themselves about evidence to be sifted at a later period.

Besides the hole through the coat-skirt, the sheriff's *posse* found nothing else that seemed to point specially towards the crime—except the double-barrelled gun. To its bore exactly fitted the bullet which the hunters had extracted from the cypress-knee, and which was now in possession of those instructed to prosecute. Woodley, however, apart, and acting on his own account, had discovered a pair of boots, heavily laden with mud, hidden away under a heap of rubbish at the bottom of an old peach orchard. The backwoodsman had surreptitiously kept these to himself,

10—2

intending to make private, and particular, use of them; his comrade, Heywood, being alone made privy to the secret of their discovery.

Having finished their investigation of the premises, the sheriff's party hurried their prisoner off to the county town; leaving his father behind in a state of terrible bewilderment, half crying, half crazily cursing.

Most of the men, hitherto following the chief officer of the law, parted with him at the plantation-gate. He and his constables were thought enough to keep charge of the accused. A sheriff in the South-western States is a very different sort of individual from the men who perform the duties of this office in the north, or the grand dignitaries, with scarce any duties at all, in a shire of England. He of the backwoods must be a man of unflinching courage—indeed, often desperate—else the mandates entrusted to him would result in a failure of justice, and a mockery of the executive power. It is rarely that they do—rare, indeed, when a Mississippian sheriff proves recreant to his trust. Far more common to find him ready to die, or at least risk death, in the performance of his dangerous duty; and not unfrequently is this the actual result. While travelling through the South-western States, I have often witnessed, and admired as well, the wonderful self-sacrificing bravery of these responsible officers of the law. Who could help admiring it?

Therefore, the party who had been with the sheriff, assisting in the arrest, saw no necessity for following him further. They had full confidence that he would deposit his prisoner within the walls of the county gaol. So, parting with him and his constables — after passing out of Darke's plantation-gate—they turned off in a different direction. Whether or not the murderer had been discovered—most of them believed he was—they had yet to search for the body of the murdered man.

Again, as on the day before, they separated into several parties—each taking a tract of the woods, though all keeping in the neighbourhood

where the blood had been spilled, and Clancy's
gun and hat found.

But their search again proved as fruitless, as on
the preceding day. More so : since on the second
scouring of the woods nothing new was discovered that could throw additional light upon
the commission of the crime, or aid them in
recovering the corpse.

Again they dragged and poled the creek up
and down, penetrating into the swamp, as far as
was possible, or likely that a dead body could
have been carried for concealment. In its deep
dark recesses they found no trace of man, either
living or dead; only the solitude-loving crane, the
snake-bird, and the scaly alligator.

It was but a poor report to take back to the
plantations; a sad one for the mother of the
missing man.

She never received it. Before the returning
searchers could speak the unsatisfactory intelligence into her ear, Mrs. Clancy lay cold in death.

The long-endured agony of ill fortune, the
more recent one of widowhood, and now this new

bereavement of a lost only son; for she fully believed him lost—basely assassinated—this accumulated anguish was too much for her woman's strength, of late fast failing. And when the neighbours got back, clustering around her dwelling, they could hear sounds within, that told of some new disaster.

On the night before they had heard the same; but now the tone was different. Then the widow's voice was lifted in lamentation; now it was not heard at all.

Whatever of mystery there might be, it soon received elucidation.

A woman, coming out upon the porch, and raising her hand in token of silence, said, in sad, solemn voice,

" *Mrs. Clancy is dead !*"

CHAPTER XVII.

WHILE search was being made for the body of the murdered man—while that of his mother, alike murdered, was lying cold upon her bed of death —while the murderer of both was cowering within the cell of a prison—a steamboat was cleaving the current of the Red River of Louisiana; slowly forging its course up stream; its single paddle-wheel—for it had only one—beating the ochre-coloured water into foam, that, floating far behind, danced and simmered upon the surface, forming a wake-way of what appeared to be blood-froth.

It was a little "stern-wheel" steamer, such as in those days plied upon many of the tributaries of the Mississippi; the impulsive power being confined to a single set of paddles, placed where the rudder acts in most other vessels, and looking very much like the wheel of an old-fashioned water-mill.

The boat in question was called the "Belle of Natchez;" perhaps somewhat pretentiously: since it was but an indifferent sort of craft—small in size, and poor in its appointments. On the particular trip of which we are speaking it might more appropriately have laid claim to the distinctive appellation; since it carried a young lady who, for some time, had borne it without denial or dispute.

The lady was Helen Armstrong, known among Mississippians as the "Belle of Natchez." By singular coincidence, the boat so designated was bearing her away from her Mississippian home— from scenes long loved and cherished; once joyful, now sad; in retrospect only sacred to the sacrifice of her heart.

Was she leaving that heart behind her? No. It was with her, within her breast; but breaking —well-nigh broken.

The "high pressure" steam-craft that ply upon the western rivers of America have but slight resemblance to the black, low-hulled leviathans that plough the waters of the Atlantic. The steamer of the Mississippi more resembles a house, rounded off at the corners to an oblong oval shape, painted snow white, two stories in height, the upper one furnished on each face with a row of casement windows, which serve also as outside doors to the state-rooms. Inside ones, opposite these, give admission to the main cabin, or "saloon," which runs midway through the boat for almost its whole length—glass folding doors dividing it into three compartments. These are the ladies' cabin aft, the dining-saloon in the centre, and a third division forward containing a "bar," used only by the male passengers, for smoking, drinking, and too often gambling.

Along the casements, opening outside, each furnished with green jalousies or Venetian shutters, runs a narrow balcony, with a low balustrade, or guard-rail, to keep a careless passenger from falling off into the flood. The same is carried round the stern of the boat, ladies' cabin included. A projection of the roof, termed the "hurricane deck," acts as an awning to this outside gallery, shading it from the sun. Two immense twin-chimneys—or "funnels," as called —stand up out of the hurricane-deck, pouring forth a continuous volume of white wood-smoke; while a third but smaller tube, termed the "'scape-pipe," intermittently vomits smoke still whiter; the steam at each emission giving a hoarse bark that may be heard for miles along the river.

On such a steamer—differing from others only in having a stern-wheel instead of side paddles —had Colonel Armstrong embarked with his family, transporting them to the "wilder west."

And up the Red River of Louisiana they were making way; slowly, as a stern-wheel boat of scarce a hundred horse-power, against a rapid and turbulent current, must needs make it.

It was the hour of night—the second after leaving Natchez—but not late. Lights gleaming from open cabin windows, or shimmering through the Venetian shutters, told that but few, if any, of the passengers had yet retired to rest. It was, in truth, but the after-tea hour, when the tables of the main saloon had been cleared, and gentlemen, as also ladies, sate around them to read; play cribbage; perhaps, take a hand at some round game of cards, as "vingt-un" or "beggar-my-neighbour." The square games—often not so square as regards the honesty of the play—were carried on in the bar-saloon, further forward.

On this particular "trip" there chanced to be many lady passengers on board the Belle of Natchez—as also several gentlemen—some of them accomplished and agreeable. For this reason the Armstrong girls had no need to be sufferers from solitude.

Notwithstanding, one of them was so—seeming to prefer it.

Is it necessary to say which? No. The reader has already guessed—Helen.

Escaping from the saloon, with its continuous hum of conversation—from speeches that but wearied, and flattery that only fashed her—

she had taken refuge on the stern-guards of the boat, abaft the ladies' cabin. Notwithstanding the hour, she there found herself alone. The other ladies had each some attraction to keep them inside — her sister a very particular one.

In Jessie's case it was a young planter named Dupré; a Louisianian Creole, who had his plantation in the neighbourhood of Natchitoches, whither the boat was bearing them. He had been to Natchez upon business, and was now returning home.

His handsome features, brunette complexion, black eyes, and gracefully-curling hair had made havoc with the heart of Jessie Armstrong, in less than twenty-four hours after their first meeting. *En revanche,* her contrasting colours of red, blue, and gold, seemed to have held their own in the amorous encounter.

So that, before the Belle of Natchez had steamed fifty miles up Red River, these two of her passengers, judging from their behaviour, showed unmistakable symptoms of making a much longer

voyage in company—in short, a journey through
life.

Colonel Armstrong took note of their " billing
and cooing," but made no objection to it. Why
should he ? The gentleman was known upon
the boat as one of the wealthiest planters
in his State; equally noted a sa noble young
fellow—brave, accomplished, and of irreproach-
able character—such as are often found among
the Creoles of Louisiana.

Jessie Armstrong had chosen well; though it
was not wealth that had influenced her choice.
Only love—intuitive, instinctive ; true love, with,
perhaps, the usual alloy of passion.

Her elder sister had no jealousy, not even
envy. The love that occupied Helen's heart—
that had torn, and left it lorn—was the one
love of a life. It could never be replaced by
another. If she had any thought about her
sister's new-sprung happiness, it was not envy at
her being happy, but sadness from its light of joy
contrasting with the shadow of her own misery.

As she stood upon the stern-guards of the

steamboat, her eyes now mechanically bent upon the revolving wheel that whipped the water into foam, now piercing the darkness beyond, she felt stealing over her a darker thought—that still more terrible than sadness—that which oft prompts to life's annihilation. The man to whom she had given her heart—its firstlings as well as fulness—a heart in which there could be no second gleanings, and she knew it—this man had made light of the sacrifice. And it was a sacrifice grand, because glowing with the whole interests of her life.

The life, too, of a woman gifted with rare excellences of spirit and person; queenly, commanding; above all, beautiful.

She did not think this about herself, as she leant over the guard-rail of the steamer. She only thought of her humiliation; of having been humiliated by him at whose feet she had flung herself; fondly, but too recklessly, surrendering that which woman holds most dear— the last syllable of rendition.

To Charles Clancy she had spoken it — in

writing only, but in terms unmistakable. The remembrance of that was now the cause of her chagrin, as of her shame.

Both might be ended in an instant. A step over the railing, a plunge into the red rolling river, a momentary struggle amidst its foaming waves—not to save life, but to destroy it—this, and all would be over! Sadness, jealousy, disappointed love—these bitter passions, and all others alike—could be ended in one little effort— a leap into oblivion!

Her nerves were fast becoming strung to the taking it. The past all seemed dark, the future still darker. For her, life had lost its fascinations, while death was equally divested of its terrors.

Suicide in one so young, so fair, so incomparably lovely, one capable of charming others, no longer to be charmed herself! Suicide, fearful to think of! And yet she was contemplating it!

She stood upon the guards, wavering, irresolute. It was no lingering love of life, nor fear of death, that caused her to hesitate. Nor yet the

horrid form of death she could not fail to see before her, sprang she but over that slight railing.

The moon was up, coursing the sky above in
full effulgence, its beams falling upon the broad
bosom of the river.   At intervals the boat, keeping the deeper channel, was forced close to either
bank.   Then, as the surging eddies set the floating, but stationary, logs in motion, the huge
saurian asleep on them could be heard giving a
grunt at having been so rudely awakened, and
pitching over into the current with a sullen
plunge.

She saw and heard all this.   It should have
shaken her nerves, and caused trembling throughout her frame.

It did neither one nor the other.   The despair
of life deadened all dread of death—even of being
devoured by an ugly alligator !

Fortunately, at that moment, a gentle hand
was laid upon her shoulder, and a soft voice
sounded in her ear.   They were the hand and
voice of her sister.

Jessie, coming out from the state-room behind,.

had glided silently up. She saw Helen prepossessed, sad, and could divine the cause. She little knew how near things had been to a fatal climax; —and dreamt not of the diversion her coming had caused.

"Sister!" she said, caressingly, "why do you stay out here? The night is chilly; and they say the atmosphere of this Red River country is full of miasma, with fevers to follow, and agues to shake the comb out of one's hair! Let us go inside, then! There's right good company in the cabin, and we're going to have a round game at cards—vingt-un, or something of the sort. Come in with me!"

Helen turned round, trembling at the other's touch, as if she had been a criminal, and it was the sheriff's hand she felt upon her shoulder.

Jessie noticed the strange, strong emotion. She could not fail to do so. Attributing it to its remotest cause, that morning confided to her, she said—

"Be a woman, Helen! a true, strong woman, as I know you are! Don't think of him any more.

There's a new world, a new life, opening to both of us. Forget the sorrows of the old, as I shall. Pluck Charles Clancy from your heart, and fling every memory, every thought of him, to the winds! I say again, be a woman—be yourself! Forget the past, and think only of the future— *of our father !"*

The words came like a galvanic shock, at the same time soft and soothing as balm. They had this effect upon the spirit of Helen Armstrong. They had touched a tender chord—that of filial affection.

And it vibrated true to the touch.

Flinging her arms around Jessie's neck, and kissing her rose-tinted cheek, she said—

" Sister, you have saved me !"

11—2

CHAPTER XVIII.

SEIZED BY SPECTRAL ARMS.

"*SISTER, you have saved me!*"

Such was Helen Armstrong's speech, as she placed her head on her sister's shoulder, and pressed that sister's cheek with lips pouring forth affection.

Returning the kiss, Jessie looked not a little perplexed. She could neither comprehend the meaning of the words, nor their choking utterance. Equally was she at a loss to account for the convulsive trembling throughout her sister's frame, while their bosoms remained in contact.

Helen gave her no time to ask questions.

"Go in!" she said, causing the other to face round, and pushing her towards the door of the state-room—"In, and set the vingt-un a-going.

I'll join you for the game by the time you've got the cards dealt."

Jessie, glad to see her sister once more in a pleasant mood, made no protest, but gleefully re-entered the cabin.

As soon as her back was turned, Helen once more faced towards the river—stepping close up to the stern guard-rail. The wheel was still re-volving its paddles as before, beating the water into bubbles, and casting the reddish-white spray afar over the surface of the stream.

Now, she had no thought of flinging herself into the seething current, though she meant doing so for something else.

" Before the game of vingt-un begins," she said, " here's a pack of cards to be dealt out—with a portrait among them."

As she spoke, she drew forth a bundle of letters —evidently old letters—tied in a ribbon of blue silk. One after another, she pulled them free of the fastening—just as if dealing out cards. Each, as it came clear, was rent right across the middle, and tossed despitefully into the stream.

At the bottom of the packet, after the letters had been all disposed of, was a photograph picture. It was a likeness of Charles Clancy, given to her on one of those days when he had flung himself appealingly at her feet.

She did not tear it in twain, like the letters; though at first this appeared to be her intent. Some thought striking her, she held it up before the moon, her eyes for a time resting upon, and closely scanning it. Strange wild memories, winters of them, seemed to roll over her face, while she thus made scrutiny of the features so indelibly engraven upon her heart. She was looking her last upon them, in the hope of being able to erase the image, as she had a determination to do.

Who can tell what was then passing within that heart? Who could describe its desolation? Certainly no writer of romance.

Whatever resolve she had arrived at, for a while she appeared to hesitate about the executing it.

Then, like an echo heard amidst the rippling

waters, came back into her ear the words spoken by her sister—

"*Let us think only of our father.*"

The thought decided her; and, stepping out to the extremest end of the guard-rail, she flung the photograph upon the paddles of the revolving wheel, as she did so, saying—

"Go there, image of one once loved—picture of one who has been false. Be crushed, and broken, as he has broken my heart!"

The sigh that escaped her, as she surrendered the bit of cardboard, was more like a scream—a cry of anguish. It had the accent that could only come from that she had spoken of—a broken heart.

As she turned away to re-enter the cabin of the steam-boat, she seemed ill-prepared for taking part, or pleasure, in a hand of cards.

And she took not either. That game of vingt-un was never played.

Still half distraught with the agony through which her soul had passed—the traces of which she knew must be visible on her face—before appearing in the brilliantly-lighted saloon, she passed round the corner of the ladies' cabin, intending to enter her own state-room by the outside door.

It was but to spend a moment before her looking-glass, to arrange her dress, the coiffure of her hair—perhaps the expression of her face—all things that to a man may appear trivial, but to a woman important—even in the hour of sadness and despair. No blame to woman for acting thus. It is but an instinct—the primary care of her life—the secret spring of her influence and power.

In repairing to her toilette, Helen Armstrong was but following the example of her sex.

She did not follow it far—not so far as to get before the looking-glass, or even inside the room. Before entering it, she made stop by the door, and stood with face turned towards the river's bank. The boat had sheered close in shore; so close that the tall forest trees shadowed her track —the tips of their branches almost sweeping the hurricane-deck.

They were cypresses, festooned with Spanish moss, that hung down like the drapery of a death-bed. One was blighted, stretching forth bare limbs, blanched white by the weather, desiccated and jointed like the arms of a skeleton.

It was a ghostly sight, and caused her a slight shivering, as under the clear moonbeams the steamer swept past the place.

It was a relief to her, when the boat got back again into darkness.

Only momentary; for then, under the shadow of the cypresses, amidst the fitful coruscation of the fireflies, she saw the face of Charles Clancy!

It was among the trees high up, on a level with the hurricane-deck.

It could only have been fancy? Clancy could not be there, either in the trees, or on the earth? The thing could only be a deception of her senses —a delusive vision, such as occurs to clairvoyantes, at times deceiving themselves.

Hallucination or not, Helen Armstrong had no time to reflect upon it. Before the face of her false lover faded from her view, a pair of arms, black, sinewy, and stiff, were stretched towards her; roughly grasped her around the waist; and lifted her aloft into the air !

CHAPTER XIX.

WHAT BECAME OF HER.

HELEN ARMSTRONG gave a shriek, as she felt herself elevated into the air, where for a time she was held suspended. Only for an instant—just long enough for her to see the boat pass on beneath. At the same instant she caught sight of her sister, as the latter rushed out upon the guards, and gave a piercing cry in reply to her own.

As she herself screamed a second time, whatever had seized her suddenly relaxed its hold; and her next sensation was of falling from a giddy height, till the fall was broken by a plunge into water. She experienced a severe shock, striking her almost senseless. She was only sensible of a drumming in her ears, a choking in the throat—in short, the sensation that precedes asphyxia by drowning.

The responsive cries given out by the two girls, and then continuously kept up by Jessie, brought the passengers rushing out of the saloon, a crowd collecting upon the stern-guards.

" Some one overboard !" was the thought, and the shout that rang through the vessel. It reached the ear of the pilot; who, instantly ringing the " stop" bell, caused the paddle-wheel to suspend its revolutions, bringing the steamer to a sudden stop. The strong current, against which the boat was at the time contending, con-tributed to its suddenness.

Meanwhile, Jessie, the only one who had wit-nessed the mysterious catastrophe, was too much awed by its mystery to give any intelligible explanation of it. She could only frantically exclaim,

" My sister ! taken up into the air ! She's now down in the water ! Oh, save her ! Save her !"

" In the water—where ?" asked a voice, whose

earnest tone spoke of readiness to respond to the appeal.

"Yonder—there—under that great tree. She was in its top first, then dropped down into the river. I heard the plunge, but did not see her after. She has sunk to the bottom. Merciful Heavens! O Helen—sister! Where are you?"

The people were puzzled by these incoherent speeches. Both passengers above, and boatmen on the under-deck, were alike mystified. They stood as if spell-bound.

Fortunately, one of the former had retained his presence of mind, and along with it his coolness. Fortunately, too, he had the courage to act under the emergency. As also the capacity, being a swimmer of the first class. It was he who had asked the question "Where?"—the young planter, Louis Dupré. He only waited to hear the answer. While it was being given, he had hurriedly divested himself of his coat and foot wear. In evening costume, his shoes were easily kicked off—white waistcoat and coat tossed aside at the same time. Then, without

staying to hear half the offered explanation, he
sprang over the guards, and swam towards the
spot pointed out.

"Brave, noble fellow!" was the thought of
Jessie, her admiration for the man—now her
acknowledged suitor—for the moment making
her forget the peril in which her sister was
placed.

But it now seemed less. Confident in her
lover's strength, believing him capable of anything, she felt almost sure that Helen would be
saved.

She stood, as did everyone else upon the
steamer, watching with earnest, anxious eyes.
Hers were more; they were flashing with wild
feverish excitement; giving glances of hope at
intervals alternating with the fixed gaze of fear
—the expression of her features changing in correspondence.

There might be wonder at her hopes, but none
at her fears. The moon had sunk to the level of
the tree-tops, and the bosom of the river was in
dark shadow; darker by the bank where the

boat was now drifting. But little chance there was to distinguish an object in the water—less for one swimming upon its surface. And then the river was deep, its current rapid, its waves turbid and full of dangerous eddies. In addition, it was a spot infested—well known to be the favourite haunt of that hideous reptile, the alligator, with the equally dreaded gar-fish—the shark of the South-western waters. All these things were in the thoughts of those who stood bending over the stern-guards of the Belle of Natchez; causing them anxiety for the fate, not only of the beautiful young lady who had fallen overboard, but the handsome, courageous gentleman who had plunged in, and was swimming to her rescue.

Anxiety would be a light word — a slight, trivial feeling—compared with that throbbing in the breast, and showing itself in the countenance of Jessie Armstrong. Hers was the torture of terrible suspense ; gradually growing into the acute agony of despair, as time passed, and the young planter returned not, nor was anything to be seen of him in the water. Then her father, standing by her side, could do little to comfort her. He, too, was paralysed—a prey to agonized emotions.

The steamer's boat had been manned, and set loose as quickly as could be done. It was now right over the spot where the swimmer had been last seen, and all eyes were fixed upon it—all ears listening to catch any word of cheer.

Not long had they to listen. From the shadowed surface of the river came a shout sent up in joyous tones,

"*She's saved !*"

Then, quickly after, spoke a rough boatman's voice,

"All right! We've got 'em both. Throw us a rope!"

The rope was thrown by ready hands, after which came the command, "Haul in!"

A light, held high upon the steamer, flashed its beams down into the boat. Lying along its thwarts could be perceived a form—that of a a lady—in a dress once white, now discoloured by the muddy water filtering from its skirts. Her head rested upon the knees of a man, whose scant garments were similarly saturated.

It was Helen Armstrong, supported in the arms of Louis Dupré.

She appeared lifeless; and the first sight of her drew anxious exclamations from those standing upon the steamer.

Only for a short while was the anxiety endured. A few minutes after she had been carried to her state-room, there came from it the report that she still lived, and was out of danger. Colonel Armstrong himself imparted to his fellow-passengers this intelligence—joyfully received by every one of them.

     *   *   *   *

Inside the state-room of the two sisters, after their father had gone forth, there was a little bit of a scene, with a conversation that may be worth repeating. The younger commenced it by saying,

" Tell me, Helen! Dear sister, don't be afraid

to speak the truth. Why did you jump over-board ?"

" Jump overboard ! What are you talking about, Jessie ?"

" I declare I don't know myself. It seems such a mystery, all of it. I saw you for some time up in the air, as if hovering there, like an angel, on wings ! I'd be willing to swear, that I saw you so. Of course, it could only have been my fancy, frightened as I was at seeing you fall overboard. After that you appeared to drop straight down, your white skirt streaming after. Then I heard a plunge. O Helen ! it was fearful ; both the fancy and the reality. What did it mean ?"

" That was just what I was asking myself at the time you saw me suspended, as you say, in the air ; for so I was, dear Jessie. I soon after-wards arrived at the explanation of it. Though puzzling me then, as it does you still, nothing can be more simple."

" But what was it, anyhow ?"

" Well, then, it was this : As I stood leaning over the guard-rail I was suddenly carried away from it, as if by a pair of strong, bony arms. After keeping me awhile, they released me from their grasp, letting me fall plump into the river, where certainly I should have been drowned but for——"

"For Louis—my dear Louis !"

"Ah ! Jessie ; I don't wonder at your admiration. He deserves it all. I am envious, but not jealous. I can never know that feeling again."

"Dear sister ! do not think of such things. Don't you see you haven't yet explained the strangest part. What carried you into the air ? You speak of a pair of arms. What kind of arms ? To whom did they belong ?"

"To a ghostly cypress-tree. Yes, Jessie ; that is the explanation of what mystifies you, as it did me for a while. I know all about it now. A great outstretching limb, forked at the end, had caught the steamer somewhere forward, and got bent down. It caught me, also, just as it was springing up again, and gave me the swing, and the drop, and the good ducking I've had. Now you know all."

A sweet joy thrilled through Jessie's heart on receiving this explanation. She was no longer troubled with a suspicion, hitherto distressing her. *Her sister had not intended suicide!*

CHAPTER XX.

THE men who, after the second day's search, had returned to Mrs. Clancy's cottage were few in number, being only her more intimate friends and well-wishers. Most of the searchers had gone direct to their own homes.

Soon, however, the news spread abroad that the mother of the murdered man was herself stricken down. This, giving a fresh stimulus to sympathy, as well as curiosity, caused all to assemble anew—many starting from the beds, to which they had betaken themselves after the day's fatigue.

Before midnight there was a crowd around the house, greater than any that had yet collected. And of the voices mingling in conversation the tone was more excited and angry. It was only subdued in the presence of that corpse, lying cold upon its couch, its pale face turned appealingly towards them.

From the dead there was no need of any appeal to cause a demand for justice. Many of the living were loudly calling for it; and close to the chamber of death, knots of men, with their heads near together, were discussing the ways and means of obtaining it, surely and quickly.

In such cases there are always some who command. It may not be from any superiority of rank or wealth. In the hour of need the rightful chieftains—those whom God designed should lead—are recognised, and acknowledged.

A group, composed principally of these, stood in front of the cottage, debating what was best to be done. It was a true backwoods jury, roughly improvised, and not confined to twelve ; for there were more than twenty taking part in the deliberation. They had drawn together by a sort of tacit and common consent, and by the same had a foreman been appointed, a planter of standing in the neighbourhood.

The question in debate was at first twofold : Had Charles Clancy been murdered ? And, if so, who was his murderer ?

The former was soon decided in the affirmative. No one had the slightest doubt about the crime. The conjectures of all were turned towards the criminal. What proof could be brought forward to fix it on the man that day arrested, and who was now lying in the gaol to await legal trial ?

Every sign seen by any of the collected crowd, every incident that had transpired, was as calmly discussed, and carefully weighed by this rough, backwoods jury, as if it had been composed of the twelve best men to be found in the most civilized city. Perhaps with more intelligence— certainly with as much determination to arrive at a righteous verdict.

They discussed not only the occurrences of which they had been made aware, but the motives that might lead to them. Among these last came prominently up the relations that had existed between the two men. There had been nothing hitherto known to tell of any hostility, that might lead to the commission of such a crime.

There was little said about Darke's relations with the family of the Armstrongs, and less of Helen Armstrong in particular. It was suspected that he had sought the hand of the young lady; but no one thought of Clancy having been his rival. Up to that time Colonel Armstrong had maintained a proud position. It was not probable he would have permitted his daughter to think of matching with a man circumstanced as was Charles Clancy.

Clancy's love secret had been carefully kept. None were privy to it. A few only suspected it —among these his mother, whose lips were now sealed by death.

Had the deliberating backwoodsmen but known that he had been Darke's rival suitor—still more, the successful one—it would have given a different turn to their deliberations—almost a key to the crime. Than such motive, nothing points more surely to murder.

Had Helen Armstrong been herself present among them, or near—anywhere that she could have had tidings of the tragical events exciting the settlement—there would have been no difficulty about their coming to a conclusion. The self-constituted jury would, in all probability, have been told something to elicit from them a quick verdict, an equally quick sentence, with, perhaps, its instant execution.

But Helen Armstrong was no longer there—no longer near. By that time she must have been hundreds of miles from the place, she and all related to her. Any secret she could have disclosed was not available for that trial going on by the widow Clancy's cottage.

And, as no one suspected her of having such secret, her name was only mentioned incidentally, without any thought of her being able to throw light upon the dark mystery they were endeavouring to make clear.

For several hours they remained in consultation, weighing the testimony that had been laid before them.

The circumstances that seemed to fix the guilt upon Darke were repeatedly passed in review, and still they did not bring conviction—at least, not complete. No one of them but might have been compatible with his innocence. A bullet fitting a smooth-bore fowling-piece, however exactly, was not of itself testimony sufficient to hang a man; even though Clancy's body had been found with the ball in it. Both these conditions were wanting to the chain of evidence. The body had not been found, and the bullet was only buried in the bark of a cypress-knee.

The blood which it had carried with it into the wood was evidence of its having first passed through living flesh—whether that of man, or animal, could not be decided.

The torn hole through the skirt of Darke's coat, connected with Clancy's gun having been found discharged, looked more like something from which a deduction could be drawn, unfavourable to the accused. Though it might also favour him, as proof of a fight between the two, and that the killing of Clancy was not a premeditated murder. Of this circumstance Darke had offered no explanation. After his arrest he had preserved a sullen silence, and refused to answer interrogatories.

" You're going to try me," he said, in reply to a question put by one of the sheriff's party. " 'Twill be time enough then to explain what appears to puzzle you."

The worst appearances against him had been his own behaviour, as also that of the dog—both, to say the least, exceedingly suspicious. About the latter he had made a statement upon the ground; though it had failed to satisfy those of the searching party who were most prone to suspect him. And, now. that time had elapsed, and they had sufficiently reflected upon it, his account of the affair seemed still less like the true one. His having once chastised Clancy's dog might, naturally enough, make the animal afterwards spiteful towards him. But why had this spite not been shown while they were around the

cottage, before setting out on the search ? Why
was it only made manifest, and in such earnest
manner, after they had arrived under the cypress
—beyond doubt the place where the dog had last
looked upon its master ?

Although still nothing more than circumstantial, to many of those engaged in the inquiry,
this chapter of testimony appeared almost con-
clusive of Darke's guilt.

During the deliberations two individuals came
upon the ground, who contributed an additional
item of information, corroborative of this. These
were Simeon Woodley and Ned Heywood.
Their added testimony referred to the footprints
seen by the swamp's edge. After assisting at the
arrest they had proceeded thither, taking Darke's
boots—which Woodley had surreptitiously secured
—along with them. Like the bullet to the barrel
of his gun, his boots were found to fit the tracks
exactly. No others could have made those
marks in the mud. So certified the two hunters, declaring their readiness to make oath of it.

It was another link in the chain of circumstantial evidence, still further strengthening the case against the accused.

As these facts were brought forward, one after another, the group of deliberators seemed gradually subsiding into a fixed belief, likely soon to end in action—that sort usually taken by the executive officers of " Justice Lynch."

CHAPTER XXI.

THE COON-HUNTER CONSCIENCE-STRICKEN.

BLUE BILL, after confiding the dread secret to his sable spouse, felt altogether easier in his mind; and having, as related, lain down by her side in the midst of his black olive branches, on that night, slept soundly enough.

As yet he had no certain knowledge, that a murder had been committed. He only knew that a fight must have taken place between two men, one of whom was his young master, and the other he presumed to be Charles Clancy. He had heard the exchange of shots, and afterwards saw the former rushing past in reckless retreat, which seemed to show that the affair must have had a tragical ending, and that Clancy had been killed. Still the coon-hunter could not know it to be so; and, hoping it might be otherwise, he was not so much frayed by the affair as to lose his night's rest.

In the morning, when, as usual, hoe in hand, he went abroad to his work, no one would have suspected him to be the depository of a secret so momentous. He was noted as the gayest of the working gang,—his laugh, the loudest, longest and merriest, carried across the plantation fields, whether among corn stalks, cotton plants, or tobacco leaves; and on that particular day, it rang with its wonted cheerfulness.

Only during the earlier hours. When at midday a report reached the place where the slaves were at work, that a man had been murdered, a white man, a neighbour who lived near by, and that this man was Charles Clancy, the coonhunter, in common with the rest of the gang, threw down his hoe, all uniting in a shout of sympathetic sorrow. For all of them knew young " Massa Clancy," most respecting, and many of them loving him. He had been accustomed to meet them with pleasant looks, and accost them with kindly words.

The sad tidings produced a profound impression upon all; and from that moment, though their task had to be continued, there was no more cheerfulness in the tobacco field. Even their conversation was hushed, or carried on in a low, subdued tone; the hoes being alone heard as their steel blades struck upon an occasional stone.

But while his fellow labourers were only silent through sorrow, Blue Bill was speechless from another and different cause. They only knew that young Massa Clancy had been killed—murdered as the report reached them — while he knew how, when, where, and *by whom*. This knowledge made him feel different from the rest; for while sorrowing as much, and perhaps more than any, for Charles Clancy's death, he had fears for his own life, and good reasons for having them.

He well knew, that if Dick Darke should become acquainted with the fact of his having been a witness to that rapid retreat among the trees, he, Blue Bill, would be speedily put where his tongue could never give testimony. In short, the coon-hunter saw that his life was in danger of being compromised by his ill luck—in being the involuntary spectator of a crime, or at least of such circumstances as would prove its committal. In full consciousness of this, he determined not to commit himself by any voluntary avowal of what he had seen, or heard; but resolved to bury the secret in his own breast, and to insist upon its being so interred within the bosom of his better half.

That day Phœbe was not in the field along with the working gang; and this gave him anxiety. The coon-hunter could trust his wife's affections, but was not so confident as to her prudence. She might say something in the "quarter" to compromise him. A word—the slightest hint of what had happened — might lead to his being questioned, and confessed—with torture, if the truth were suspected.

No wonder that during the rest of the day

Blue Bill wore an air of abstraction, and hoed the tobacco plants with a careless hand, often chopping off the leaves. Fortunately for him, his fellow slaves were not in a mood to observe these vagaries, or make inquiry as to the cause.

He was rejoiced when the sound of the evening bell summoned them back to the " big house."

Soon he was once more in the midst of his picaninnies, with Phœbe by his side; to whom he imparted a fresh caution to "keep dark on dat ere seerous subjeck."

They talked over the events of the day—Phœbe being the narrator. She told him of all that had happened—of the search, and such incidents connected with it as had reached the plantation of the Darkes; how both the old and young master had taken part in it, both having returned home. She added, of her own observation, that Massa Dick looked " berry scared-like, an white in de cheeks as a ole she-possum."

"Dats jess de way he oughter look," was Blue Bill's response. After which they ate their frugal supper, and once more went to rest.

But on this second night the terrible secret, shared by them, kept both from sleeping. Neither got so much as a doze.

And as morning dawned, they were startled by hearing noises in the negro quarter. They were not the usual sounds consequent on the uprising of their fellow slaves; a commingling of voices, in jest and cheerful laughter. On the contrary, it was a din of serious significance, with cries that told of calamity.

When the coon-hunter drew back his door and looked forth, he saw commotion outside; and was soon told its cause. One of his fellow bondsmen coming forward, said :—

"Mass Dick am arrested by de sheriff. Dey tuk 'im for de murder ob Mass Chal Clancy."

The coon-hunter rushed out, and on to the big house. He reached it in time to see Richard Darke set upon a horse, and taken off to the county jail. Then, with a feeling of relief, he returned to his Phœbe.

"Now," he said to her, "dar ain't no longer so much reezun to hab fear. I see Sime Wood-

13—2

ley mong de men; and dis nigger know dat he'll gub me his proteckshun, whatsomever I'se do. So, Phœbe gal, I've made up my mind to make a clean bress ob de hul ting, and tell what I heern an see, besides deluverin' up boaf de letter an de picter. What's yar view ob de matter? Peak plain, and doan be noways mealy-mouthed 'bout it."

"My views is den, for de tellin' ob de troof. Ole Eph Darke may flog us till dar ain't a bit o' skin left upon our backs. I'll take my share ob de 'sponsibility an half ob de floggin'. But let de troof be tole—de whole troof, an nuffin but de troof."

"Den it shall be did. Phœbe, you're a darlin'. Kiss me, ole gal. If need be, we'll die togedder."

And the two black faces came in contact, their bosoms, too—both beating with a humanity that might shame whiter skins.

CHAPTER XXII.

A VOLUNTARY WITNESS.

WHILE the improvised jury was still in consultation and yet undecided, the little clock on the mantel struck twelve midnight; of late not oft a merry hour in the cottage of the Clancys, but this night more than ever sad.

The striking of the clock seemed the announcement of a crisis. For a time it silenced the voices of those conversing, both inside the house and out.

And scarce had the last stroke ceased to vibrate on the still night air, when a voice was heard, that had not yet taken part in the deliberations. It sounded as coming from the road gate.

"Mass Woodley in da?" spoke the voice,

interrogatively; the question addressed to. the group gathered in front of the house.

"Yes; he's here," simultaneously answered several.

"Kin I peak a wud wif you, Mass Woodley?" again asked the inquirer at the gate.

"Sartinly," said the hunter, separating from the others, and striding towards the road entrance.

"I reck'n I know that voice," he added, on drawing near. "It's Blue Bill, ain't it?"

"Hush, Mass Woodley! For Goramity's sake doan peak out ma name. Not fo' all de worl let dem people hear it. Ef dey do, dis nigga am a dead man."

"Why, Bill; what's the matter? Why d'ye talk so mysteerous? Is thar anythin' wrong? Oh! now I think o't, you're out from the quarter arter time. Never mind 'bout that; I'll not betray you. But what hev ye come for?"

"Foller me, Mass Woodley; I tell yer all. I dasent tay hya, lees some ob dem folk see me. You kum little way from de house, into de wood groun; den I tell you wha fotch me out. Dis nigga Bill hab somethin say to you berry patickler. Yes, Mass Woodley, berry patickler. 'Tam a ting ob life an def."

Woodley did not stay to hear more; but, lifting the latch, quietly pushed open the gate and passed out into the road. Then following the negro, who flitted like a shadow before him, the two were soon standing under cover of some bushes that formed a strip of thicket running along the road-side.

"Now, what air it?" asked Woodley of the coon-hunter, whom he well knew from having often met him in his midnight rambles.

"Mass Woodley, you wants know who kill Mass Charl Clancy?"

"Why, Bill, that's the very thing we're all talkin' 'bout, an' tryin' to find out. In coorse we want to know. But who is thar to tell us?"

"Dis nigga."

"Air ye in airnest, Bill?"

"So much in earness dat I ha'n't got no chance go sleep till I hab reveal de seecret. De ole

ooman neider. No, Mass Woodley, Phœbe she no
let me ress till I do dat same. She say it am de
duty ob a Christyun man, an', as ye know, we
boaf b'long to de Methodies. Darfore, I now tell
ye, de man who kill Charl Clancy wa my own
massr—de young un—Mass Dick."

"Bill! are ye sure o' what ye say?"

"So shoo I kin swa it as de troof, de whole
troof, an' nuffin but de troof."

"But what proof have ye?"

"De proof! I most seed it wif ma own eyes.
If I didn't see, I heerd it wif ma ears."

"By the 'tarnal! this looks like clar evydince
at last. Tell me, Bill, o' all that you seed an' what
you heern?"

"Ya, Mass Woodley, I tell you ebberyting; all
de sarkimstances c'nected wif de case."

In ten minutes after, Simeon Woodley was
made acquainted with everything the coon-hunter
knew; the latter having given him full details of
all that had occurred on that occasion when his
coon-chase was brought to such an unsatisfactory
termination.

To the backwoodsman it was not a surprise. He had already arrived at a fixed conclusion, and Bill's revelation was in correspondence with it.

On hearing it, he but said—

" While runnin' off, yur master let fall a letter, did he ? You picked it up, Bill ? Ye've got it?"

" Hya's dat eyedentikil dokyment."

The negro handed over the epistle, the photograph still inside it.

" All right, Bill ! I reckon this oughter make things tol'ably clar. Now, what dy'e want me to do ?"

" Lor, Mass Woodley ! You knows bess. I'se needn't tell ye dat. Ef ole Eph'm Darke hear wha dis nigga hab been an' gone an' dud, de life ob Blue Bill wuldn't be wuth a ole coon-skin— no ; not so much as a corn-shuck. I'se get de cowhide ebbery hour ob de day and de night too. I'se get flog to def, sa'tin shoo."

" Yur right thar, I reckon," rejoined the hunter ; and then continued, reflectingly, " Yes ; you'd be sarved putty sevâre if they war to know on't. Wal, it mustn't be, and won't be—that I

promise ye, Bill. Your evydence wouldn't count
for anythin' in a law court, nohow. Tharfor, we
won't bring ye forrad; so don't you be skeeart.
I guess we shan't want no more testymony, and
thar ain't likely to be any cross-kwestenin' law-
yers in the case. Now, d'you slip back to yur
quarters, and gi'e yurself no furrer consarn. I'll
see you shan't git into any trouble. D——d ef
I don't!"

With this emphatic promise, the old deer and
bear-hunter separated from the less pretentious
votary of the chase; as he did so, giving the
latter a squeeze of the hand, which told him he
might go back in confidence to the negro-quarter
and sit by the side of his Phœbe without fear.

CHAPTER XXIII.

CONVINCING EVIDENCE.

WITH impatience the backwoods jury awaited the return of the backwoodsman. With impatience; for, before his leaving them, they had well-nigh resolved upon a verdict, with a sentence, and the mode of carrying it into execution. One after another had stepped across the threshold of the cottage, entered the chamber of death, and looked upon the corpse of Clancy's mother—whom they all regarded as having been murdered, as much as her son.

And one as another, after gazing on that pale face, that seemed making its mute appeal to them for justice—for vengeance—came out muttering a vow, that there should be both : some loudly vociferating it, with the emphasis of an oath.

It did not now need what Simeon Woodley
had in store to excite them to instant action.
Already were they sufficiently inflamed. The
furor of the mob, with all its maddened vengeance, had been gradually permeating their
spirit, and had almost reached its culminating
point.

Still had they sufficient calmness to keep them
patient a little longer, and hear what Woodley
might have to say. They knew, or suspected,
that he had been called from them on some
matter connected with the subject under conside-
ration. At such a time who would have dared
interrupt their deliberations for any trivial purpose ? Although none of them recognised Blue
Bill's voice, adroitly disguised as it had been,
they knew it was that of a negro. This, however, was no reason why the hunter should not
have received some communication likely to
throw fresh light on the affair. So, once more
gathering around him, they demanded to know
what it was; then respectfully listened.

He told them all he had heard, without making

known who was his informant, or in any way compromising the brave fellow with a black skin, who had risked life itself by making disclosure of the truth.

To this the old hunter only referred in a slight manner. They all understood its significance, and none pressed him for more minute explanation.

"My informant," he said, after finishing the chapter of occurrences communicated by the coon-hunter, "has gived me the letter dropped by Dick Darke, which, as I've told ye, he picked up. Here it air. Preehaps it may throw some more light on the matter; though I guess you'll all agree wi' me that the thing's clar enough a'ready."

They all did agree. A dozen voices had repeatedly declared, were still declaring that. Some now cried out—

"What need to talk any more? Charley Clancy's been killed—he's been murdered. Dick Darke's the man that did it!"

It was not from any lack of convincing evidence, but rather a feeling of curiosity, that prompted them to call for the reading of the letter, which the hunter now held conspicuously in his hand. Its contents might have no bearing upon the case. Still there could be no harm in knowing what they were.

" You read it, Henry Spence! You're a scholart, an' I ain't," said Woodley, handing the letter over to a young fellow of learned look—the schoolmaster of the settlement.

Spence, stepping close up to the porch, into which some one had carried a candle, and holding the letter before the light, first read the super-scription, which, as he told them, was in a lady's handwriting.

" *To Charles Clancy,*" he said.

" Charles Clancy !"

Half a score voices pronounced the name, all in a similar tone—that of surprise. One asked,

" Was that letter dropped by Dick Darke ?"

" It was," said Woodley, to whom the question was addressed.

" Have patience, boys !" urged an elderly

man. " Don't interrupt till we hear what's in it."

They all took the hint, and remained silent.

But when the envelope was laid open, and a photograph drawn out, showing the portrait of a young lady, recognised by all as a likeness of Helen Armstrong, there was a fresh outburst of exclamations betokening increased surprise; which became stronger still, when Spence read out the inscript upon the picture :

" HELEN ARMSTRONG, FOR HIM SHE LOVES."

The letter was addressed to Charles Clancy; to him the photograph must have been sent! A love affair between Miss Armstrong and the man who had been murdered! A new revelation to all present; astounding as significant!

" Go on, Spence! Give us the letter!" called an impatient voice.

"Yes, give us the letter! We're on the right track now, I reckon," added another.

The epistle was taken out of the envelope. The schoolmaster, unfolding it, read aloud :—

" Dear Charles,—

" When we last met under the magnolia, you asked me a question. I told you I
would answer it in writing. I now keep my
promise, and you will find the answer underneath
my own very imperfect image, which I herewith
send inclosed. Papa has finally fixed the day of
our departure from the old home. On Tuesday
next we are to set out in search of a new one.
Will it ever be as dear as that we leave behind ?
The answer will depend upon—need I say whom ?
After reading what I have written upon the
carte, surely you can guess. There, I have
confessed all—all woman can, could, or should.
In six little words I have made over to you my
heart. Accept them as its surrender !

" And now, Charles, to speak of things more
prosaic, as in this hard world we are constrained
to do. On Tuesday morning—at a very early
hour, I believe—a boat will leave Natchez, bound
up the Red River. Upon it we travel as far as
Nachitoches. There we are to remain for some
time, while completing preparations for our

farther transport into Texas. Father is not certain what part of the 'Lone Star' State he will select for our future home. He speaks of a place upon some branch of the Colorado River, said to be a beautiful country; which you, having been out there, will know all about. In any case, we are to remain for a time—at least six weeks— in Nachitoches; and there, *Carlos mio*, I need not tell you, there is a post-office for receiving letters, as also for delivering them. Mind, I say for *delivering* them! Before we leave for the far frontier, where there may be neither post-office nor post, I shall write you full particulars about our intended 'location'—with directions how to find it. Need I be very minute? Or can I promise myself, that your wonderful skill as a 'tracker,' of which we've heard, will enable you to discover it? They say Love is blind. I hope, dear Charles, yours will not be so: else you may not find the way to your sweetheart in the wilderness.

"How I go on talking, or rather writing, things I intended to say to you at our next meeting under the magnolia — our magnolia! Sad thought this, tagged to a pleasant expectation: for it must be our last interview under the dear old tree. Our last anywhere, until we come together again in Texas—perhaps on some prairie where there are no trees. Well; we shall then meet, I hope, never more to part; and in the open daytime, where we shall need neither night, nor tree shadows to conceal us. I'm sure father, humbled as he now is, will no longer object. Dear Charles, I don't think he would have done so at any time, but for his reverses. They made him think of—never mind what. I shall tell you all under the magnolia.

"And now, master mine—this makes you so— be punctual! Monday night, and ten o'clock— the old hour. Remember that next morning I shall be gone, long before the wild wood songsters are singing their '*reveillé*' to awake you. Jule drops this into our tree post-office to-night— Saturday night. You have told me you go there every day. Then you will be sure of getting it in time; and once more I may listen to your flattery, as you quoted the old song about 'showing the night flowers their queen.'

"Oh! Charles, how sweet that was, is, and ever will be, to yours,

"HELEN ARMSTRONG."

"And that letter was found on Dick Darke?" questioned a voice, as soon as the reading had come to an end.

"It war dropped by him," answered Woodley; "and tharfor ye may say it war found on him."

"You're sure of that, Simeon Woodley?"

"Wal, a man can't be sure o' a thing unless he sees it. I didn't see it myself wi' my own eyes. For all that, I've had proof clar enough to convince me; an' I'm reddy to stan' at the back o' it."

"D——n the letter!" exclaimed one of the impatient ones, who had already spoken; "and the picter, too! Don't mistake me, boys. I ain't referrin' eyther to the young lady as wrote it, nor him she wrote to. I only mean that neither letter nor picter are needed to prove what we're

14—2

all wantin' to know, an' do know. They arn't nor warn't reequired, nohow. To my mind, from the fust go off, nothin' ked be clarer than that Charley Clancy has been killed, 'cepting as to who killed him—murdered him, if ye will; for that's what's been done. Is there a man on the ground who don't know the name o' the murderer?"

The interrogatory was answered by a unanimous negative, followed by the name, "Dick Darke."

And along with the answer commenced a significant movement throughout the crowd. Threats were heard—some muttered, some spoken aloud—while men where observed looking to their guns, and striding towards their horses; as they did so, crying sternly, "To the gaol! to the gaol!"

In ten minutes after these horses were in motion, with riders upon their backs, moving along the road between Clancy's cottage and the county town. They formed a cavalcade, if not regulat in line of march, terribly imposing in aspect.

Could Richard Darke, inside the cell where he

was confined, have seen those marching horsemen, heard their threats, and witnessed their
excited gestures, he would have shaken in his
shoes, and with a trembling worse than any ague
the swamp fever could have given him.

CHAPTER XXIV.

TO THE GAOL.

THE gaol in which Richard Darke had been incarcerated was, as we have said, in the capital town of the county where the murder—if murder it was—had been committed.

In the old civilised countries of Europe the phrase "county town," or "capital of the county," presents an imposing idea. There rises before the fancy an array of streets, generally crooked, with several crossings, a market-house, one or more churches, and, it may be, a cathedral.

A county town in the Southern or South-western States of America, need not suggest any parallel to this picture. True, some may show streets crossing, but never crooked; certainly the churches in more than the Old-World proportion;

and indubitably a building of far greater pretension than the English town-hall or market-house.

This will be the "Court-House"—a structure almost peculiar to the American Republic, and forming a conspicuous feature in the national architecture ; as it also plays an important part in the political life of the country.

I have no space, nor need it be my purpose, to depict an American Court-House, or the many uses to which it is put. Sufficient to say that, notwithstanding its great size and pretentious style of architecture—sometimes the grandest Grecian, with Corinthian columns and swelling cupola—it frequently stands in the centre of a town that could scarce claim to be called village —a mere collection of "weather-boarded" houses, suburbed by log cabins, not much better than huts.

The "Hotel" is the only other building in the place that dares look at the Court-House, and say, "I am a house as well as you."

In point of size and grandeur, it is justified in

making this defiance; for in the smallest American town there is sure to be an "hotel" capable of bedding a hundred guests—if a Court-House town, two hundred—and dining them at the same table.

The reason for the county towns of the United States being thus often insignificant places is well understood. It is simply the result of a law—a sequence of Republican faith and fairness—that the political centre of any district shall be placed in a central situation, territorially, so as to be equally accessible to all. This spot, however accommodating to legislators, is often the reverse for the convenience of its inhabitants, its commerce, and generally the industrial development of the place. The consequence is that the county town has a lively-deadly existence, remaining stagnant for a long period of time; its latest and only progress being that which it saw when first founded —when the Court-House was erected, and the half-score of frame-buildings, with the hotel, shot up simultaneously. The log cabins may have been there before.

Such a county town was that in whose gaol Richard Darke had been lodged. A Court-House in the centre, with plenty of open space around it; the "Hotel" standing opposite, a wooden structure, painted white, with an array of windows and green venetian shutters, numerous as in a spinning factory; twenty or thirty private dwellings, similarly limned; a livery stable; two or three stores; and a straggling suburb of "shanties," surrounded by a rank vegetation of "jimson weeds" and wild pennyroyal. The county gaol was a part of the Legislative building, situated in a sort of wing projecting from the main structure. There was but one room, or cell, devoted to this special purpose; for in the South-western States only a desperate criminal —a man committed for murder or some capital crime—could be shut up in a prison cell. For the detention of debtors, there was another and better style of chamber, in a remote corner of the Court-House.

It was close upon two o'clock a.m. on the morning after Dick Darke had been placed in confinement, when the troop of horsemen, already described, was seen approaching the county town by one of the roads that led to it. They were still riding straggled out, and irregularly, to all appearance without leader or anyone commanding them. Notwithstanding this, there was an idea or purpose, that seemed to inspire and keep them in a sort of order. At all events, it carried them straight on, and with as much decision as though they were moving by the strictest military discipline.

When close up to the Court-House, and opposite the door of the gaol, they halted without having received any word of command, though as promptly as if this had been given by the most martinet colonel.

And, on halting, every one of them leaped out of his saddle; threw the bridle rein over its bow; left the horse to take care of itself; but holding on to the gun each had in hand.

Thus they advanced toward the cell, in which the accused had been the day before shut up.

Three or four of them, some a little in advance

of the others, who had already arrived at the door, were seen standing by it in attitudes and with looks that betokened surprise.

There should, then, have been a gaoler to receive them. There was none!

So much the better, thought some; it would be all the easier to accomplish the purpose for which they had come.

This was to break open the prison door, drag out the incarcerated criminal, and *hang him*— without further trial, either by judge or jury. " Lynch " had already pronounced the sentence ; they, his executive officers, were then to carry it into execution.

Strange that the gaol-keeper should not be at his post! Was he in connivance with them, and had withdrawn to give a good opportunity? Or had he been warned of their approach, and, knowing their desperate design, forsaken his post through fear?

Whatever the reason, he was not there—neither he nor anyone representing him. There was nothing to stay them in their intent. Nor was there any authority that could have done this. No power, not even the sheriff with his posse. At that moment it would have been dangerous for any man, or party of men, to have offered obstruction to the stern, determined officers whom Justice Lynch had deputed to carry out his decree.

From him they had the order to take Dick Darke from his prison, and hang him forthwith. No special place was mentioned. The nearest post, or tree-branch—for that matter, the swing sign of the hotel. Anywhere; so long as the criminal was executed.

With this resolve, fixed before their starting from Mrs. Clancy's cottage, and kept firm by frequent threats and angry ejaculations as they journeyed along the road, they broke open the door of the prison, and rushed into the cell, where they knew, or supposed, the malefactor to be confined.

Some prudent ones remained by the door, to prevent his egress. Others went inside to seize him.

The chamber was dark and silent. When a light had been struck, *they saw that it was empty !*

For once the decree of Judge Lynch remained null and void. Richard Darke, a sure assassin, had escaped from the vengeance of angry executioners.

CHAPTER XXV.

A CHOICE OF SONS-IN-LAW.

ABOVE two hundred miles from the mouth of
Red River—the Red of Louisiana—stands the
town of Nachitoches. The name is Indian, and to
be pronounced as if written "Nak-e-tosh." It is
one of the oldest of South-western settlements—
dating from the earliest attempts at Spanish and
French colonisation in the Mississippi valley;
having at different periods been in possession of
both nations; finally falling to the United States,
at the transfer of the Louisiana territory, in 1803,
by Napoleon Bonaparte.

For eighteen millions of dollars, which would
not at the present time purchase a single parish
in Louisiana State, Bonaparte, pressed for money,
surrendered a tract of territory since transformed

into several populous provinces—in fact, most of
the North American continent between the
Mississippi River and the Rocky Mountains : for
it was through the cession of Louisiana that this
became claimable by the Government of the
United States.

From its early colonisation by two distinct
branches of the Latinic race, and its after-occupa-
tion by the commingling of many nationalities
that compose the American people, the population of Louisiana presents to the ethnologist a
study of peculiar interest—the negro and native
Indian also forming an element in the amalgam.

In Nachitoches the traces of these varied
types of humanity still exist, with many of the
peculiar national customs appertaining to each:
though not so distinctly marked as some twenty
odd years ago, when it was the scene of certain
incidents now to be recorded in our story. Then,
was it a place fully deserving to be called *peculiar;* that is, when compared with most other
American towns—especially those of the north.
It was, in fact, only a large village; but as unlike

a village on the Susquehanna, Hudson, Merrimac, or Connecticut, as a Swiss hamlet to a conglomeration of smoking factories in Massachusetts or Lancashire.

Standing upon a bluff of the Red River's bank, elevated many feet above the water surface, its painted wooden houses, built French fashion, with verandahs—there called "piazzas"—and high-pitched roofs, its trottoirs brick-paved and shaded by trees of almost tropical foliage—conspicuous among them the odoriferous magnolia, and the *melia azedarach,* or "Pride of China"—these in places completely arcading the streets—the town of Nachitoches offered the aspect of a *rus in urbe,* or *urbs in rure,* whichever way you may wish it. The porches and piazzas were entwined with creepers; here and there were stretches of trellis, along which meandered the cord-like tendrils of bignonias, aristolochias, and orchids, their flowers drooping over doorways, shutting out the too bright sunlight from windows, and filling the air with fragrance; while among them whirred the tiny humming-bird, buzzed the large humble-bee, or from one to another, on silent wing, flitted the butterfly. These were sights you saw at every turning, as you made promenade through the streets of Nachitoches.

And there were other sights equally gratifying to the eye. In these same trellised verandahs you saw young girls of graceful mien, elegantly apparelled, lounging in the open porches, or, perhaps, peering coyly through the half-closed jalousies, their eyes invariably dark brown or coal black, the marble forehead above them surmounted with a chevelure in hue resembling the plumage of the raven. For at that time most of the demoiselles of Nachitoches were descended from the old Latinic colonists—the Saxon blonde having scarce yet shown herself in the far South-west.

Meet these same young ladies in the street, it was the custom, and *comme il faut*, to take off your hat, make a bow, and pass on—of course without stopping. Every man who claimed to be a gentleman was expected to do this; and every woman, whether lady or not, if decently dressed, was treated to such deference. On which side or other the privilege might be supposed to lie, it was denied to none. The humblest shop clerk or artisan—even the dray-driver—might thus make obeisance to the proudest and daintiest damsel who trod the trottoirs of Nachitoches. It gave no right of converse, nor the slightest claim to acquaintanceship. A mere formality of politeness; and to presume carrying it further would not only have been deemed a rudeness, but instantly, and perhaps very seriously, resented.

At the time spoken of, there appeared upon the streets of this polished Southern town two young ladies, to whom hats were taken off with more than the usual alacrity, and bows made with an obsequiousness, as also an elaborate grace, that in many cases spoke of an inner prompting beyond mere politeness. The ladies in question were sisters, who had lately arrived in the place, and were staying at its principal hotel. There was no mystery in Nachitoches as to who they were, nor need there be any here. They had not been forty-eight hours in the town before every young "blood" belonging to it, and every planter or planter's son within a circuit of twenty miles, knew them to be the daughters of Colonel Archibald Armstrong—late of Mississippi State, and now on the way to establish himself in Texas.

The adverse fortunes of the Mississippi planter soon became equally well known : though, so far as his daughters were concerned, it need not have affected their future. For that matter neither needed to go on into Texas. Before their father had been ten days in Nachitoches, he might have made choice of sons-in-law to the number of at least a dozen, all eligible; among them a member of Congress, two or three of the State Legislature, a couple of officers quartered at the nearest military post, with an assortment of planters, wealthy merchants, and men who made their living by the law.

These suitors were all rejected—all except one. The young planter, by name Louis Dupré, already spoken of as having laid siege to the heart of Jessie Armstrong, had finally stormed, and

15—2

captured it. The most important question of his life had been asked; the answer of most importance, to hers, as well as his, had been given. Vows had been exchanged between them.

The younger daughter of Colonel Armstrong had not surrendered unconditionally. Before leaving the old home, she had promised her father she would not forsake him—at least not till they had become settled in their new one. Louis Dupré was told of this promise; and signified his assent to its conditions, in a way that not only met every obstacle, but made things mutually agreeable to himself and his future father-in-law. This he did, by proposing to accompany the latter into Texas, and bear a part in the fortunes of the projected settlement. The Creole planter could yield this point all the more easily, as, in common with many other Louisianians, he had already been turning his eyes towards that splendid territory, recently acquired from the Sister Republic of Mexico.

Dupré had triumphed over many rival aspirants

to the affections of Jessie Armstrong; for many there had been.

They were few, however, compared with the host making suit to her who was to be his future sister-in-law. About Helen Armstrong the *jeunesse doré*—the "bloods"—of Nachitoches were, many of them, half mad. Within a week after her arrival, two or three duels were fought on her account, fortunately without fatal ending.

Not that she had given anyone the slightest cause, or cue, to be her champion. She had favoured no one with even so much as a smile. On the contrary, she had met all their approaches with a denying indifference; while a cloud of melancholy seemed to brood almost continuously on her brow. .

Anyone might have perceived that there was *un verme rongeur*—a worm eating at her heart. Too plainly was she suffering from a passion of the past.

This did not dismay her Nachitoches adorers; nor hinder them from continuing their adoration.

On the contrary, it only deepened it; her cold indifference setting their hot Southern hearts aflame—its very chillness but maddening them the more.

CHAPTER XXVI.

NEWS FROM NATCHEZ.

ABOUT ten days had elapsed since the arrival of
Archibald Armstrong and his people in Nachitoches. The colonel had been, all the intervening time, engaged in getting up a party for
his proposed colonisation in Texas. A grand in-
crease of strength had been gained, by the acces-
sion of Dupré, the betrothed of his daughter
Jessie. The young planter possessed wealth in
abundance, plenty of cash in hand, with a
numerous belonging of slaves—these of all ages
and shades of colour, from negro black to quadroon
white. He had also stock and chattels in correspondence.

On the score of decadence, or bankruptcy,
there was no necessity for him to break up his

Louisiana home. This was only being done for the reasons already assigned—one of them being the condition imposed by his *fiancée*. On her part it was not caprice, nor was it called forth by any frivolous pretext. He knew this, and admired her all the more. He knew she was but keeping that vow made to her father, sacred as any oath, on the day when Richard Darke was rejected by her sister; and repeated on another day, when Ephraim Darke sent word to Archibald Armstrong in the shape of a legal summons, to turn out from his home, forfeited by the foreclosing of the mortgage. Then, Helen Armstrong had once more made promise not to forsake her father, but to bear part in his misfortunes, until such time as he might recover from them; then Jessie, with equal zeal and like filial affection, had joined in the resolve. All this the latter had made known to her affianced, by way of excusing herself for what might otherwise have appeared a too harsh, or vexatious condition.

She had no need to have given the explan-

ation.   To the young Creole, love-entranced, any
conditions would have seemed easy: so long as
they made him sure that the blonde beauty was
to be his.   Besides, as we have said, he had
already been casting his thoughts towards
Texas; inspired by that restlessness peculiar to
Western and South-western men—ever impelling
them on either southward, or towards the setting
sun.

Louis Dupré, moreover, had certain other ideas
of his own, conceived in a spirit of ambition.   He
had travelled in Europe—in France; with some
of whose noblest families he held relationship—
since from one of them was he descended.   In
Louisiana he was but a planter among planters.
In Texas, where land was cheap, he had a dream
of establishing himself on a grander scale—at
least as regarded territory—in short, of founding
a sort of Transatlantic *seigneurie.*

For this Colonel Armstrong would be no weak
ally.   The late Mississippian planter, though in
reduced circumstances, was still held in high
estimation.   His character commanded respect;

and would be sure to draw around him some of those strong, stalwart men of the backwoods, equally apt with axe and rifle, without whom no settlement on the far frontier of Texas would stand a chance of either security or success.

For it was to the far frontier they intended going, where land was still sold at Government prices: a dollar and a quarter—five English shillings the acre !

Now that Louis Dupré, a capitalist, had joined it, the organisation of the intended colony was easy enough ; and Colonel Armstrong had but to superintend the preparations—the purchase of waggons, with their teams of mules or oxen ; the engagement of teamsters and other attendants ; as also some examination into the character, and credentials, of families proposing to be their fellow-colonists.

In these various duties the colonel was thrown a good deal upon himself, and his old campaigning experiences. Beyond the fact, that his future son-in-law would be sure to provide the sinews of war, he received but slight assistance from him, either in planning the expedition or carrying out its details.

On his side, the careless Creole was too much engrossed with his golden-haired Jessie to give thought to anything else. She was the sunbeam in which he basked, and out of her presence he felt as if in shadow. Her absence was uncongenial to him, as night to the helianthus. Even in her company, if others were present, there was constraint to him, and perhaps also to her. Both liked being alone—*chez eux mêmes*—as Dupré, speaking his native language, used jestingly to say, when they had the good fortune of being by themselves.

As a consequence of this dual selfishness, Helen Armstrong was often left without company, or with only that of her mulatto maid, Julia. . The girl observed the signs of grief visible on the brow, and pressing upon the heart of her young mistress. She could only guess at its cause; though she could do this with a good deal of certainty. Jule had been instructed to read; and, when she used to drop those scented billets-doux into the knot-hole of the magnolia, she not only knew them to be love-letters, but also the name of the man who was expected to take them from their place of deposit.

Of the last letter she had there carried, and what it had led to, her young mistress had not made her acquainted—even of as much as was known to herself. This was only what had been told her by Darke, at that ill-starred nocturnal encounter under the shade of the same magnolia.

The tragical incidents that took place afterwards were, to the maid as to the mistress, altogether unknown. No news of them had as yet reached Nachitóches.

Not from these, then, came that deep melancholy, at times bordering on despair; and which the proud lady, stricken in her most sensitive part, endeavoured to conceal, even from her slave, whom habit had taught her to regard as one would a wall, a tree, or a dumb animal.

But the mulatto girl, bondswoman though she was, possessed a heart brimful of affection—more especially for her whose waiting-maid she was. She had been deeply penetrated by the sorrow she saw weaving its spell round the life of her young mistress, threatening to destroy it. Jule had her own sorrows to endure — her lover left behind—she, and only one other, as she supposed, knew where. Jupiter, the run-away, of her own race, colour, and kind, a slave like herself, was far away, in all likelihood still lurking in the dismal recesses of the swamp. But she was sustained by the hope, that he might yet escape from his difficulties, and rejoin her in a land where the dogs of Dick Darke would no longer be able to track him. Whatever might be the fate of the fugitive slave, she was sure of his devoted love for herself, and this was sufficient to keep her from despairing. Therefore, had she the strength and spirit to sympathise with her white mistress, whom she saw, day by day, endeavouring to bear up, but evidently sinking.

Jule could not look upon these signs, without making an effort to ascertain the true cause. The time had come for knowing it. It was not curiosity, but a nobler sentiment, that prompted her.

Inspired by this, she entered the chamber of Helen Armstrong when the latter was alone. She carried in her hand that which she believed would give her the clue to her young mistress's melancholy. It might, perhaps, still further deepen it.

"See, Miss Helen?" she said, stepping across the room with an agitated air, "here's a Natchez newspaper just come by the post. It has something in it, I'm sure will be news to you, but sad news, I fear."

The young lady stretched forth her hand and took hold of the newspaper — the *Natchez Courier*. Her fingers trembled as they closed upon the sheet. At the same time her eyes blazed up with a fierce jealous light. She expected to read among its marriage notices that of Charles Clancy with a Creole girl, whose name was unknown to her. It would be the latest chapter, the culminating point, of his perfidy.

Oh! what a change came over her counten-

ance, when, instead of his marriage, her eye
rested upon a heading that proclaimed — *his
murder !*

After that, change succeeded change in the
glances of her eyes, the colour of her cheeks, her
air, attitude, everything, as, with palpitating
heart and quick-beating breast, she drank in the
details given by the newspaper—set, as they
were, in conspicuous type.

They told of the murder of Charles Clancy;
of the arrest of Richard Darke, as the suspected
murderer; and of the latter having been taken
to the gaol of the county town. There was
nothing said of what had been done to him after
—the paper having gone to press on the day of
the arrest.

It contained, however, an account of the death
of Clancy's widowed mother, and the consequent
excitement throughout the settlement where
these tragical events had taken place. Other
details were given; and one paragraph of special,
of terribly painful interest, to Helen Armstrong—
holding her spell-bound as she read it.

It is scarce necessary to say, that this related to the letter she had herself written, addressed to Charles Clancy, and by Richard Darke abstracted from the tree.

Its contents were only given in epitome, as a copy of it had not reached the hands of the editor. But, even thus, they were compromising to her; fearfully humiliating, and she felt it.

The sadness had been enough, without the shame. Both together were beyond bearing; and the proud girl, hitherto sustained by an indignant jealousy, now gave way to a different emotion. Letting fall the paper upon the floor, she sank back into her chair, her heart wildly beating within her breast—threatening to beat no more.

CHAPTER XXVII.

SPECTRES IN THE STREET.

THE Nachitoches Hotel, at which Colonel Armstrong had put up before starting out on his expedition to Texas, was, as a matter of course, the principal one in the place. It would not have been proper for a planter—even a decayed one—to stay at a second-class house.

The first was far from splendid. Compared with one of the princely hostelries of the present day—set beside that, the princeliest of them all, the "Langham" of London—it would have appeared a hut alongside a palace.

Yet was it in every way comfortable. What it might lack in interior luxuriousness—as regarded upholstery and the like—was fully compensated by its outside adornings; these not owing aught

to the architecture of the house, but all to the
vegetation that surrounded and shadowed it.
The native magnolia spread its broad laurel-like
leaves against the painted wooden walls, while
the exotic " Pride of China," rivalling the indi-
genous tree both in flower and fragrance, let fall
its perfumed spikes against the green jalousies ;
as if courting admiration from those who sate
within the chambers, into which were wafted its
delicious odours.

On a still spring night, with a full moon coursing through southern skies, when the gleam of
the fireflies could only be perceived under the
darker shadow of the trees, two ladies might
have been seen inside the vine-trellised verandah
of the quaint, old-fashioned, wooden house, which
was then the chief hotel of Nachitoches. The
ladies in question were both young; and the
moonbeams shimmering through the lattice-work
showed they were both beautiful—of the two
distinct styles, brunette and blonde. To be sure
of this, it will be sufficient to say, they were
Helen Armstrong and her sister Jessie.

On the faces of the two, thus differing in complexion, still more different was the expression. On Jessie's dimpled cheeks danced gladness, joy sparkling in her eyes of greyish blue. For her the past had no sorrows, the future no fears. Her life was in the present—the bright, prosperous present. She dwelt upon the sunny side of the cloud, amidst its silver lining. She was at that moment expecting her lover, Louis. He had promised to come; and, with the instinct of a woman, knowing herself well beloved, she had no fear of his disappointing her.

How different with her sister! Different in everything,—memories of the past, thoughts of the present, forecasts for the future. The sheen of her raven hair, the sombre shadow on her brow, her wan cheeks already beginning to show signs of wasting, the look of settled hopelessness in her eyes, once so grandly, so imperiously glancing,—all this was in contrast with the countenance of her sister.

She had reason for being sad. The disappointments, chagrins, sorrows, that within a short

16—2

period of time she had been called upon to endure, were enough to prostrate the proudest spirit, and bring it to a level with the earth.

And along with all these, thrown into the scale, was the shame of that letter, the contents of which would be scattered abroad, and known everywhere.

It was not of the letter she was now thinking. No. Little would she have cared for any humiliation it could have caused, had Charles Clancy been still alive. It was his death that was giving her the great grief—that, and a thought of the wrong she had done him. The two combined, made up an agony lacerating her heart—almost cleaving it in twain.

"Cheer up, Helen! Cheer up, dear sister! Remember that many others have had to suffer the same as you."

These were the words of Jessie.

The response :—

"No, never! Or, if many have, none to recover from it. How could they? We women, Jessie —true women, like you and myself—have but

one love in our life. If we lose that, we can
have no other, or none worth having. I have
lost it, and care not to live an hour longer."

" No, no, no ! Do not talk that way ; you distress me, sister. Pray do not speak so. Time
will change everything—time and our new life
in Texas. Your sadness will depart, and all will
be well again. I feel sure of it. There is joy
yet in store for you There is, Helen ! there is !"

" Never—for me, never !"

The chill, determined rejoinder had its effect.
Jessie, awed by it, desisted from her attempt at
consolation. She saw it was of no use just then ;
and a delicate instinct admonished her to post-
pone the task for a more favourable opportunity.

Besides, she was then expecting her own lover,
who might make his appearance at any moment.

He had not yet entered the hotel. She knew
this, for she had been watching the approaches to
it, the street running right and left. At intervals she had been scanning it through the lattice-work, scrutinising the street promenaders,—

herself unseen, screened by the leafy climbing-plants, the bignonias, with their bell-shaped flowers, and the odoriferous aristolochias.

Once more she placed herself at the post of observation, and looked along the street. She took note of every passenger that passed under the arcade of the China trees, endeavouring to identify a certain form and set of features. Only those of masculine gender were submitted to her scrutiny. To the women that went past, white or black, she scarce gave a glance. The men alone had any interest for her, and of them only one—Louis Dupré. So she believed, as, in the shadowy verandah, she stood awaiting him, thinking of no one else.

She was mistaken. Just at that moment some one else came in sight—one in whom she had an interest, or rather for whom she had a fear—something more, a feeling of repulsion.

It was a man of colossal size, who was seen silently gliding along the trottoir, under the shadow of the trees.

He stopped in front of the hotel, just opposite

the verandah, and stood gazing at her, as she leant over the baluster rail.

Even about this man's figure there was something forbidding — an expression of slouching brutality. But it was nothing, compared with the sinister cast seen upon his features, as they appeared under the light of a lamp that flared from the entrance-door of the hotel.

Jessie Armstrong, recognising the face, did not stay to scrutinise it. The recognition was instantaneous, and caused her to tremble and shrink back. Quickly receding beyond eyeshot from the street, she placed herself in a cowering attitude by the side of her sister.

"What's the matter, Jess?" asked Helen, observing her frayed aspect, and in turn becoming the comforter. "You've seen something to vex you? Something of—Louis?"

"No, no, Helen! Not him."

"Not him! Some one else? Who?"

"Oh, sister!" responded Jessie, "it's a man fearful to look at. A great big fellow with features that would frighten anyone. I've met him several times, when out walking alone. Every time I see him it sends a shiver through me. I cannot tell why."

" Has he been rude to you ?"

" Not exactly rude, but certainly something like it. I might say impertinent. He stares at me in a strange way from under a broad-brimmed hat, pulled low over his eyes. And such eyes ! They look hollow and horrid, like those of an alligator. I saw them just now, as he was passing, and stopped under the lamp-light. I believe he's standing there still."

" Let me have a peep at his alligator eyes. Perhaps I can give them such a look, in return, as for the future may make the fellow better keep his distance."

The fearless elder sister, more defiant through her very sadness, stepped forward to the veran-dah railing, and, leaning over it, looked down into the street.

She saw people passing—several men; but none that would answer to the description given by her sister.

One, however, came past, whose gait first, and then his figure, and after that his face, attracted her attention—attracted and strongly arrested it.

He, too, stopped in front of the hotel. Foolishly, if he had any occasion for concealing his face. Since, in the position he had assumed, the lamplight fell full upon it. Well might he have wished it otherwise : for in the countenance so presented Helen Armstrong identified features that exposed their owner to danger, while at the same time causing terror to herself.

She stood as if overpowered, fascinated by the sight. It was a strong, terrible emotion that held her so transfixed.

And only for an instant. Then, recovering herself, she retreated backwards, intending to take counsel with her sister.

Jessie was no longer there. Her lover had meanwhile entered the hotel, and she had silently glided from the verandah to receive him.

In its shadow Helen was alone, appalled by

the loneliness, her heart beating audibly within her breast.

And for some time she stood thus—despite her boasted courage, trembling. She, too, had been frayed by a spectre in the street.

On scanning the piazza, she saw that there was no human figure in it, save her own. She had seen this on first stepping back, and only looked mechanically.

There was light enough to make discernible the outlines of a chair—the cane-seated rocking-chair of the States. Into this she sank, without thought of its power of oscillation, or availing herself of it. On the contrary, she remained rigidly erect upon the seat, with the chair poised as upon a pivot, in balance.

Her thoughts were similarly concentrated; her hands clasped over her forehead, as if to keep them from scattering.

On stepping back from the balustrade, she had done so with a feeling of alarm, and a shiver throughout her frame. What she had seen was well calculated to cause both.

Both were over in an instant, her courage and coolness returning : along with them an impulse of anger.

Down in the street, at less than twenty paces distant, was the assassin of her lover—the man who had made her life desolate. There was he, after escaping from the prison in which his cap tors had confined, and so negligently guarded, him. She had now the news of his escape, by a later mail that had arrived at Nachitoches.

She could have him re-arrested—could, should, and would. This was the resolve to which she came, after the first moment of confusion.

But how ? At once cry "murderer !" and call upon the street passengers to seize him ?

No. It would be the very way to give him a chance of getting off. Ere the cry could be responded to, he would be away into the woods, with sufficient start not to be easily overtaken. Around Nachitoches the thickest kind of timber, almost untouched by axe, came close up to the houses. Within a hundred yards of the outskirts a man might plunge into the primeval forest—a fugitive find concealment in thicket and swamp.

Helen Armstrong was over twenty years of age ; had been brought up in the backwoods, accustomed to western ways. Of enterprising spirit, like the pioneer stock from whom she was descended, reflective and inquiring, she also understood something of western wiles. She had the sense, and *sang-froid*, to take the necessary steps for counteracting them. She saw that by raising an illjudged outcry, she would be only giving the criminal a chance to escape from the justice he had already once baffled.

As he had not seen, or, at all events, not recognised her—she imagined this—there could be no need for any hurried action to prevent his leaving the place. Doubtless, he would be there for days. One, or less—half a day, an hour—would be enough to carry out the purpose that now shaped itself in her thoughts. This was to communicate what she had seen to her father, as also to Louis Dupré—leaving them to take steps, for the re-arrest of the gaol-breaker.

Than this she could not then have done more. For on returning to look upon the street—her natural courage having overcome the fear that had for a moment overpowered her—she saw that the spectre had disappeared. Concealed by the vine-laden trellis, she stood for some time gazing along the *trottoir*, scanning it in both directions as far as the lamps illumined it. Far off, on the dim edge, where light became blended with darkness, she thought, or fancied, she could still trace the outlines of him, whom she knew to be the assassin of her lover.

Whether his or not, the man so observed was in the act of moving away. He was already too far off to be hounded with a " hue-and-cry," that would give any chance of overtaking, much less making capture of him.

But this Helen Armstrong had no longer thought of raising. She resolved on the other course of action. To carry out which she only waited for the return of her father—at the time absent from the hotel—and the disentanglement of Louis Dupré from his amorous dalliance with her sister.

" Where is the woman ?" ("Où est la femme ?") was the first question asked by Talleyrand, when any knotty point of national policy was brought before him. The famed diplomatist knew, and acknowledged, he had no adversaries in his own line more difficult to deal with than women. Nor yet more frequently; since, according to his interrogatory, there was sure to be one at the bottom of every trouble—the *causa teterrima belli.*

Talleyrand's faith has not always been found true. In the case of Helen Armstrong, feminine diplomacy was destined to defeat. On seeing Richard Darke in the street, better had she at once shouted " murderer." It might, perchance, have led to his re-arrest. As it was, the result was very likely to be different : since other eyes, besides hers, were engaging in a little bit of by-play, watching both. They were those described by her sister as resembling the eyes of alligators.

The owner of them, after what he had seen, came to certain conclusions; these being such, that he stole silently away from the spot, determined to put the assassin upon his guard.

CHAPTER XXVIII.

THE "CHOCTAW CHIEF."

"You'll excuse me, stranger, for interruptin' you in the readin' o' your newspaper. I like to see men in the way o' acquirin' knowledge. But we're all of us here goin' to take a drink. Won't you join?"

The invitation, rudely if not uncourteously extended, came from a man of middle age, who stood at least six feet three, without counting the thick soles of a pair of horseskin boots—the tops of which rose several inches above his knees. He was a person rawboned and generally of rough exterior, wearing a blanket coat; his trousers tucked into the aforesaid boots, with a leather belt round his waist, under the coat, but over the haft of a bowie-knife, alongside which peeped out the brass butt of a Colt's revolving pistol—army pattern. In correspondence with this paraphernalia of clothing and equipment, he showed a cut-throat countenance, typical of the State Penitentiary; cheeks bloated as from excessive indulgence in drink; eyes watery and somewhat bloodshot; lips thick and sensual; with a nose set obliquely, looking as if it had received hard treatment in some pugilistic encounter. His hair was of a yellowish clay colour, of lighter tint over the eyebrows. There was none either on his lips or jaws, nor yet upon his thick hog-like throat, which seemed as if some day it might stand in need of something stiffer than a beard to protect it from the noose of the hangman.

He, to whom the invitation had been extended, was of quite a different appearance; not a whit less repulsive, only that the repellant points were mental or moral, rather than physical. In age he was not much over half that of the individual who had addressed him—twenty-five, perhaps—of dark complexion, tint cadaverous; the cheeks haggard, as if from sleepless anxiety; the upper lip showing elongated bluish blotches, as from a pair of moustaches recently removed; the eyes coal black, with a sinister glance, sent with suspicious furtiveness from under a broad hat-brim pulled low down over the brow. His figure might have been well enough, but for garments somewhat coarse and clumsily fitting; too ample both for body and limbs, as if intended to conceal these, rather than show them to advantage.

A practised detective, after scanning this individual, taking note of his habiliments, especially his hat and the manner of wearing it, would have pronounced him a person dressed in disguise—a disguise, for some strong reason, adopted. A thought, or suspicion, of this kind appeared to be in the mind of the rough Hercules who had invited him to drink; though *he* was no detective.

"Thank you," said the young fellow, lowering the newspaper to his knee, and raising the rim of his hat as little as possible; "I've just taken a drink. I hope you'll excuse me."

"No; d—d if we do! Not this time, stranger. The rule o' this tavern is, that all in the bar takes a 'smile' thegither — leastwise on first meetin'. So, say what's to be the name o' yer licker."

"Oh! in that case I'm agreeable," rejoined the newspaper reader, laying aside his reluctance, and along with it the paper—at the same time getting upon his feet. Then, stepping up to the bar, he added, in a tone of seeming frankness :—

"Phil Quantrell ain't the man to back out where there's glasses going. But, gentlemen; as I'm the stranger in this crowd, I hope you'll let me pay for the drinks."

The men thus addressed as " gentlemen" were seven or eight in number; not one of whom, from external appearance, could lay claim to the epithet. So far as this went, they were all fit company for the brutal-looking bully in the blanket-coat who had opened the conversation. Had Phil Quantrell addressed them as " black-guards" he would have been nearer the mark. Villainous scoundrels they appeared, one and all:

though of different degrees as to scoundrelism in their countenances, and with a like variety of villain semblance in their costumes.

"No—no!" shouted several, determined to prove they were at least gentlemen in generosity. "No stranger can stand treat here. You must drink with us, Mr. Quantrell."

"This score's mine," said the first spokesman, in an authoritative voice. "After that anybody as likes may stand treat. Come, Johnny! trot out the stuff. Brandy smash for me."

The bar-keeper thus appealed to—as repulsive-looking as any of the party upon whom he was called to wait—with that dexterity peculiar to his craft, soon furnished the counter with bottles and decanters containing several kinds of liquors. After which he set a row of tumblers alongside, corresponding to the number of those designing to drink.

And soon they were all drinking; each having chosen the tipple most preferred by his palate.

It was a scene of every-day occurrence, every hour, almost every minute, in a tavern bar-room

of the Southern United States; the only pecu-
liarity in this case being, that the tavern in
which it took place was very different from the
ordinary village inn, or roadside hotel. It stood
upon the outskirts of Nachitoches, in a suburb
known as the "Indian quarter;" sometimes also
called "Spanish town"—both names having
reference to the fact, that the queer cabin cot-
tages around were inhabited by pure-blooded
Indians and half-breeds, with poor whites of
Spanish extraction—the last being degenerate
descendants of those who had originally colonised
the place.

The tavern itself, bearing an old weather-
washed swing-sign, on which had once been de-
picted an Indian in full war-paint, was known
as the "Choctaw Chief." It was kept by a man
supposed to be a Mexican, but might have been
anything else; who had for his barkeeper the
afore-mentioned "Johnny," a personage supposed to be an Irishman, but of like dubious
nationality.

The Choctaw Chief took in travellers; giving

them bed, board, and lodging. It usually had a goodly number under its roof; though they were travellers of a peculiar kind—strange both in aspect and manners—no one knowing when or whence they came, or at what time or whither bent, when they took their departure.

As the house stood out of the ordinary path of town promenaders, in an outskirt scarce ever visited by respectable people, no one cared to inquire into the character of its guests, or aught else relating to it. To those who chanced to stray in its direction, it was known as a sort of cheap hostelry, that gave shelter to all sorts of queer customers—hunters, trappers, small Indian traders, returned from an expedition on the prairies; and along with these, such travellers as were without means to stop at the more pretentious inns of the village; or, having the means, preferred, for reasons of their own, to put up at the Choctaw Chief.

Such was the reputation of the hostelry, at whose drinking bar stood Phil Quantrell—so calling himself—with the men to whose boon

companionship he had been so brusquely introduced; as their chief spokesman said, according
to the custom of the establishment.

The first drink swallowed, Quantrell called for
another round; and then a third was ordered,.
by someone else, who paid, or promised to pay
for it.

A fourth "smile" was insisted upon by another
someone who said he would pay for it; all the
liquor, up to this time consumed, being either
cheap brandy or " rot-gut " whisky.

Quantrell, now fairly in his cups, and acting
under the generous impulse they had produced,.
sang out, " Champagne !"—a wine which the
poorest tavern in the Southern States, even the
Choctaw Chief, could plentifully supply.

After that the choice vintage of France, or its
gooseberry counterfeit, flowed freely; Johnny
showing no reluctance in stripping the silver
necks, twisting the wire, and letting fly the
corks. For the stranger guest had taken a purse
from his pocket, which all could see was " chock
full " of gold " eagles," some observing—but say-

ing nothing about—the singular contrast of this wealth with the cheap coarse attire upon his person.

After all not much. Within the wooden walls of the Choctaw Chief there had been seen many a contrast quite as curious. Neither its hybrid landlord, nor his barkeeper, nor its guests were likely to take note—or, at all events, make remarks upon—many circumstances which else- . where would have seemed singular.

Still was there one among the roystering crowd who took note of this; as also of other acts done, and sayings spoken, by Phil Quantrell in his cups. This was the Colossus who had introduced him to the jovial company, and who still stuck to him as his chaperon.

Some of this man's associates, who appeared on familiar footing, called him " Jim Borlasse ;" others, less free, addressed him as " Mister Borlasse ;" while still others, at intervals, and rather as if by a slip of the tongue, gave him the title " Captain."

Jim, Mister, or Captain Borlasse—whichever

designation he deserved—throughout the whole debauch, kept his bloodshot eyes fixed upon their new acquaintance, and watched his every movement. His ears, too, were open to catch every word Quantrell uttered, weighing well its import.

For all this, he said, or did, nothing to show he was thus attentive to the stranger—as first his guest, but now a spendthrift host to him and his party.

While the champagne was being freely quaffed, of course there was much conversation, and on many subjects. But one became special; seeming more than all others to engross the attention of the roysterers under the roof of the Choctaw Chief.

It was a murder that had been committed in the State of Mississippi, near the town of Natchez; an account of which had just appeared in the local journal of Nachitoches. The paper was lying on the tavern table; and all of them who could read had already made themselves acquainted with the particulars of the crime. Those, whose scholarship did not extend so far, had learnt them at secondhand from their better-educated associates.

The murdered man was called Clancy—Charles Clancy—while the murderer, or he under suspicion of being so, was named Richard Darke, the son of Ephraim Darke, a rich Mississippi planter.

The paper gave further details : that the body of the murdered man had not been found before the time of its going to press ; though the evidence collected left no doubt of the foul deed having been done ; adding, that Darke, the man accused of it, after being arrested and lodged in the county gaol, had managed to make his escape —through connivance with his gaoler, who had also disappeared from the place. The paragraph likewise mentioned the motive for the committal of the crime—at least, as it was supposed or conjectured; giving the name of a young lady, Miss Helen Armstrong, and speaking of a letter and picture dropped by the suspected assassin. It wound up by saying, that no doubt both prisoner and gaoler had G. T. T.—" Gone to Texas "—a phrase at that time of frequent use in the States

—applied to fugitives from justice. It wound up by giving the copy of a proclamation from the State authorities, offering a reward of two thousand dollars for the apprehension of Richard Darke, and five hundred dollars for Joe Harkness—this being the name of the conniving gaol-keeper.

While the murder was being canvassed and discussed by the drinkers in the bar-room of the Choctaw Chief—a subject that seemed to have a strange fascination for them,—Borlasse, who had become elevated with the alcohol, though usually a man of taciturn habit, broke out with an asseveration that caused surprise to all, even his more intimate associates.

" D—n the luck !" he vociferated, bringing his fist down upon the counter till the decanters danced under the concussion; " I'd a given a hundred dollars to 'a been in the place o' that fellow Darke, whoever he is !"

" Why ?" interrogated several of his confrères. "Why, Jim ?" " Why, Mr. Borlasse ?" " Why, Captain ?"

" Why ?" echoed the man of many titles, again
striking the counter, and causing decanters and
glasses to jingle. " Why ?   Because that Clancy
—that same Clancy—is the skunk that, before a
packed jury, half o' them yellar-bellied Mexikins, in the town of Nacogdoches, swore I stoled
a horse from him.   Not only swore it, but war
believed; an' got me—me, Jim Borlasse—tied for
twenty-four hours to a post, and whipped into
the bargain.   Yes, boys, whipped!   An' by a
d—d Mexikin nigger, under the orders o' one o'
their constables, they call algazeels.   I've got the
mark o' them lashes on me now, and can show
them, if any o' ye hev a doubt about it.   I ain't
shamed to tell *you* fellows; as ye all know
what it means, I guess.   But I'm burnin' mad
to think that Charley Clancy's escaped clear o'
the vengeance I'd sworn again him.   I knew'd
he was comin' back to Texas, him and his.
That's what took him out thar when I met him
in Nacogdoches.   I war waitin' and watchin' till
he shed come this way.   Now, it appears, somebody has spoilt my plans—somebody o' the name

of Richard Darke. An', while I envy this Dick Darke, I say d—n him for doin' it."

"D—n Dick Darke! D—n him for doin' it!" rang out the chorus of roysterers, till the walls of the Choctaw Chief re-echoed the blasphemous acclaim.

*   *   *   *   *

The drinking debauch was continued till a late hour, Quantrell paying shot for the whole party. Maudlin as most of them had become, they still wondered that a man so shabbily dressed could command so much cash and coin. Some of them were no little perplexed by it.

Borlasse was, perhaps, less so than any of his companions. He had noted certain circumstances that gave him the explanation; one, especially, that seemed to make everything clear. As the stranger, calling himself Phil Quantrell, stood by his side, champagne glass in hand, he took out a pocket-handkerchief to wipe the wine from his lips. The handkerchief fell upon the floor, Borlasse picking it up, but without restoring it to its owner.

He did so, after a time; but not till he had made himself acquainted with a name embroidered on one of its corners.

When, at a later hour, the two sat together, drinking a last good-night draught, Borlasse placed his lips close to the stranger's ear, and said, in a whisper,—

"Your name is *not* Philip Quantrell: it is *Richard Darke!*"

CHAPTER XXIX.

THE MURDERER UNMASKED.

HAD a rattlesnake sounded its harsh "skirr" under the chair on which the stranger was sitting, he could not have shown more alarm, or started up more abruptly, than he did when Borlasse said—

"*Your name is* NOT *Philip Quantrell: it is Richard Darke!*"

For Richard Darke in reality it was.

He first half rose from his seat; then sat down again; all the while trembling in such fashion that the wine went over the edge of his glass, wetting the sanded floor of the bar-room.

Fortunately for him, the rest of the company had retired to bed, it being now a very late hour

of the night—near midnight. The drinking
"saloon" of the Choctaw Chief was quite
emptied of its inebriated guests—the two principal entertainers alone staying. Even Johnny,
the bar-keeper, had gone kitchenwards—in all
likelihood to look after his supper.

Otherwise the startled demeanour of the
gentleman hitherto figuring as Phil Quantrell
would have attracted eyes upon, and perhaps
brought around, him an inquisitive crowd.

As it was, there was only Borlasse to bear
witness to the effect of his own speech; which,
though but whispered, had proved so significantly
startling.

The speaker, on his side, showed no surprise.
Throughout all the evening he had been taking
the measure of his man, and had arrived at a full
comprehension of the case. He saw that he was
in the company of Charles Clancy's murderer.
The disguise that Darke had adopted—the mere
shaving off his moustaches and putting on a
dress of home-woven "cottonade"—the common
wear of the Louisianian Creoles—with a broad-

brim palmetto hat to correspond, was too thin, too flimsy, to deceive a man like Borlasse, himself accustomed to travesties and metamorphoses far more ingenious. To have appeared in keeping with his coarse garb, Darke should have shown less free of his golden coin. Though it might not have much mattered. The man into whose company he had chanced—like himself a traveller staying at the Choctaw Chief—would have seen through the thickest mask he could have assumed. It was not the first time for Jim Borlasse to meet a murderer fleeing from the scene of his crime—stealthily, disguisedly making way towards the boundary line, between the United States and Texas—towards the Sabine river, then the limit of executive justice.

"Come, Mr. Darke," he said, extending his arm in a gesture of reassurance, "don't waste the wine in that ridikilous fashion. You and I are alone, and I reckin we understand one another. If not, we'll soon come to do so—the sooner by your puttin' on no nonsensical airs, but tellen' me the clar and candid truth. First, then, answer

me the questyun: Air you, or air ye not, Richard
Darke? If ye air, don't be afeerd to say it. No
humbuggery, now! That won't do for Jim
Borlasse."

The disguised assassin, still trembling, for a
moment hesitated to make reply.

Only for a moment. He saw it would be of
no use denying his identity. The man who had
questioned him—of colossal size and ruffian
aspect—notwithstanding the copious draughts he
had swallowed during the night, seemed cool as
a tombstone, and stern as an inquisitor. The
bloodshot eyes, watery though they were, looked
upon him with a leer that said: "Tell me a lie,
and I'll be your enemy, even to stabbing you,
some time, in the dark, or shooting you down,
now, upon the spot."

At the same time those horrid eyes spoke of
safety; if the truth were told, of friendship;
such friendship as may be felt between two
criminals equally steeped in crime.

The assassin of Charles Clancy—now for many
days and nights wandering the earth, a fugitive

from foiled justice, taking untrodden paths, hiding in holes and corners, at last seeking shelter under the roof of the Choctaw Chief because of its repute for harbouring such as he —seemed at length to have reached the true haven of safety.

So thought he himself, after listening to the appeal of his boon companion, and gazing into the eyes of the man as he made it.

The volunteered confessions of Borlasse—the tale of his hostility to Charles Clancy and its cause—were enough to give Darke confidence about any revelations he might make in return. Beyond all doubt his new acquaintance stood in mud, deep as himself. Without further hesitation, he said,

"I *am* Richard Darke."

"All right!" was the reply. "And now let me tell you, I like your manly way of answerin' the question I put ye. Same time, I may as well remark, 'twould a been all one if ye'd sayed *no!* This child hain't been hidin' half o' his life, 'count o' some little mistakes made at the

18—2

beginnin' of it, not to know when a man's got
into a sim'lar fix. First day you showed your
face inside the Choctaw Chief I seed thar war
something amiss; tho', in course, I couldn't gie
the thing a name, much less know twar that
ugly word which begins with a M. This evenin',
I acknowledge, I war a bit put out—seein' you
round thar by the hotel, spyin' after one of
, them Armstrong girls; which of them I needn't
say."

Darke started, muttering, mechanically, " You
saw me there ?"

" In course; how could I help it—bein' there
myself, on the same errand, I suppose ?"

" Well ?" interrogated Darke, waiting for the
other to proceed.

" Well; that, as I've said, some leetle bam-
boozled me. From your looks and ways since
you first came hyar, I guessed that the something wrong must be different from a love scrape.
Besides, a man stayin' at the Choctaw Chief, and
sporting the cheap rig as you've got on, wan't
likely to be aspirin' to sech dainty damsels as

them. You'll give in, yourself, it looked a leetle queer, didn't it?"

"I don't know that it did," was the reply, pronounced doggedly, and in an assumed tone of devil-may-careishness.

"You don't! Well, I thought so, up to the time o' gettin' back to the tavern hyar—not many minutes afore my meetin' and askin' you to jine us in drinks. If you've any curiosity to know what changed my mind, clarin' up the whole thing, I'll tell ye."

"What?" asked Darke, scarcely reflecting on his words.

"That ere newspaper you war readin' when I gave you the invite. I read it *afore* you did, and had ciphered out the whole thing. Puttin' six and six thegither, I could easy make the dozen. The same bein', that one of the young ladies stayin' at the hotel is the Miss Helen Armstrong spoke of in the paper; and the man I observed watchin' her is Richard Darke, who killed Charles Clancy—*yourself!*"

"I—I am—I won't, I don't deny it to you,

Mr. Borlasse. I am Richard Darke. I did kill Charles' Clancy, though I do deny having *murdered* him."

"Never mind that. Between friends, as I suppose we can now call ourselves, there need be no nice distinguishin' of terms. Murder or manslaughter, it's all the same, when a man has a motive sech as yourn. An' when he's druv out o' the pale of what they call society, an' hunted from the settlements, he's not like to lose the respect of them who's been sarved the same way. Your bein' Richard Darke an' havin' killed Charley Clancy, in no ways makes you an enemy o' Jim Borlasse—except in your havin' robbed me of a revenge I'd sworn to take myself. Let that go now. He's dead; and d—d, I 'spose, by this time. I ain't angry, but only envious o' you, for havin' the satisfaction of sendin' the skunk to kingdom come, without givin' me the chance. An' now, Mister Darke, what do *you* intend doin'?"

The question came upon the assassin with a sobering effect. His copious potations had hitherto kept him from reflecting. It was only on his boon companion clearly showing a knowledge of his identity, that he felt a renewal of his fears; though they were soon after tranquillised by the "thieves' confidence" with which Borlasse now inspired him.

The interrogatory relating to his future again brought its darkness, with all its dangers, before him; and he paused before making response.

Without waiting for it, his questioner continued,

"If you've got no fixed plan of action, and will listen to the advice of a friend, I'd advise you to become *one o' us.*"

"One of you! What does that mean, Mr. Borlasse?"

"Well; I can't tell you here," rejoined Borlasse, in a subdued tone. "Desarted as this bar-room appear to be, it's got ears for all that. I see that curse, Johnny, creepin' about, pretendin' to be lookin' after his supper. If he knew as much about you as I do, you'd be in limbo afore you ked get into your bed. I needn't tell you thar's a reward offered; for you seed that yourself in the newspaper. Two thousand dollars for you, an 'five hundred dollars for the fellow as I've seed along wi' you, and who I'd already figured up as bein' gaoler Joe Harkness. Johnny, an' a good many more, would be glad to go halves with me for tellin' them only half of what I now know. *I* ain't goin' to betray you. I've my reasons for not doin' so. After what I've said, I reckon you can trust me."

"I can," answered the assassin, heaving a sigh of relief.

"All right, then," said Borlasse; "we understand one another. But it won't do to stay talkin here any longer. Let's go up to my bedroom. We'll be safe there; and I've got a bottle of brandy, the best stuff for a nightcap. Over that we can talk things straight, without anyone having the chance to set them crooked. Come along !"

Darke, without protest, responded to the invitation. He dared not do otherwise. It sounded more like a command. The man extending it had now full control over him—could at any moment deliver him up to justice—have him dragged to a gaol.

Without another word, he followed Borlasse to his bedroom.

CHAPTER XXX.

"WILL YOU BE ONE OF US ?"

As soon as the stalwart ruffian had entered his sleeping-apartment, pointed out a chair to his invited guest, and planted himself upon another —with the promised bottle of brandy between them—he resumed speech.

"I've asked you, Mr. Darke, to be one o' us. I've done it for your own good, as you ought to know without my tellin' ye. Well; you asked me in return what that means; didn't ye ?"

"Yes, I did," said Darke, answering without any definite idea or purpose.

"It means, then," continued Borlasse, taking a gulp out of his glass, "that me, an' the others you've been drinking with, air as good a set of fellows as ever lived. That we're a cheerful party, you've seen for yourself. What's passed this night ain't nowheres to the merry times we spend upon the prairies out in Texas—for it's in Texas we live."

"May I ask, Mr. Borlasse, what business you follow ?"

"Well; when we're engaged in business, that's mostly horse-catchin'. We rope wild horses, or mustangs, as they're called, an' sometimes them that ain't jest so wild. We bring them into the settlements for sale. For that reason we go under the name of 'mustangers.' Between whiles, when business isn't very brisk, we spend our time in some of the Texas towns—them what's well in to'rds the Grand River, whar there's a good sprinklin' of Mexikins in the population. We've some rare times among the Mexikin girls, I can assure you. You may take Jim Borlasse's word for that, mayn't you ?"

"I have no reason to doubt it," answered Darke.

"Well, I needn't say more, need I ? I know you're fond of a pretty face, with black eyes in it. You'll get both among the saynoritas, to your heart's content. Enough, maybe, to make you forget the pair I saw glancin' on you out of the hotel gallery."

" Glancing on me ?" exclaimed Darke, showing surprise, not unmixed with alarm.

" Glancin' on you ; right on ye."

" You mean——"

" I mean Miss Helen Armstrong's eyes ; the same that made you do that little bit of shootin', with Charles Clancy for a target."

"Do you think she *saw* me ?" asked the assassin, with evidently increasing uneasiness, and without waiting for the conclusion of the other's speech.

"Think ! I'm sure of it. More than saw—she recognised ye. I could tell that from the way she shot back into the shadow. Did ye not notice it yourself?"

" No," answered Darke, the monosyllable issuing mechanically from his lips, while a fresh chill ran through his frame.

His questioner, observing these signs, said,

"Take my advice, and come with us fellows to Texas. Before you're long there, the Mexikin girls will make you stop moping about Miss Armstrong. After the first *fandango* you've been at, you won't care a straw for her. Believe Jim Borlasse, when he tells ye you'll soon forget her."

"Never!" exclaimed Darke, in the fervour of his passion—thwarted though it had been—forgetting the danger he was in.

"If that's your detarmination," returned Borlasse, "an' you've made up your mind to keep Miss Armstrong in sight, you won't be likely to live long. As sure as you're sittin' thar, afore breakfast time to-morrow mornin' the town of Naketosh 'll be too hot to hold ye."

Darke started up from his chair, as if *it* had become too hot to remain seated on.

"Keep cool, Phil Quantrell!" apostrophised the Texan. "No need for ye to be alarmed now. There would be, if you were in that chair, or this room, eight hours later. I won't be myself, not six. For I may as well tell ye that Jim Borlasse, like yourself, has reasons for shiftin'

quarters from the Choctaw Chief. He'll be gone
a good hour afore sun-up. An' he gives you a
friend's advice, to make tracks along wi' him.
Will you go ?"

Darke even yet hesitated to give an affirmative
answer. His love for Helen Armstrong—wild,
wicked passion though it might be—was the
controlling power of his life. The thought of
leaving her behind—separating from the place in
which she stayed, perhaps never to see her again
—this thought was more repugnant, more domi-
nating, than that peril which plainly stared him
in the face—the spectre of a scaffold!

The Texan ruffian guessed the cause of his
irresolution. More than this, he understood and
knew he had the means to put an end to it. A
word would be sufficient; or, at the most, a single
speech. He spoke it thus,

"If you're determined to stick by the apron-
strings o' Miss Helen Armstrong, you'll not do
that by staying here in Naketosh. Your best
place, to be *near her*, will be along *with me.*"

"How so, Mr. Borlasse ?"

" You ought to know, without my tellin' you
—a man of your 'cuteness, Quantrell! You say
you can never forget the oldest of that pair o'
girls. I believe you; and will be candid, too, in
sayin', no more is Jim Borlasse like to forget the
youngest. I thought nothin' could a fetched that
soft feelin' over me. 'Twant likely, after what
I've gone through in my time. But she's done
it—them blue eyes of hers, d——d if they hain't!
Then, do you suppose that I'm goin' to run away
from, and lose sight o' her and them? No; not
till I've had her within these arms, and tears out
o' them same peepers droppin' on my cheeks.
That is, if she take it in the weepin' way."

" I don't understand," stammered Darke.

" You will in time," rejoined the ruffian; " that
is, if you come with us, and go where we're
goin'. Enough now for you to be told that, *there
you will find Helen Armstrong !*"

Without waiting to watch the effect of his last
words, the tempter continued,

" Now, Richard Darke, are you willin' to be
one of us ?"

" I am !"

*   *   *   *

It was late when Colonel Armstrong returned
to his hotel, and Louis Dupré became disengaged
from his *tête-à-tête* with Jessie.   Then they were
told of the spectres seen in the street; but too
late to take any steps that night for the recapture
of Charles Clancy's murderer.   Neither was per-
sonally concerned in the affair, beyond the common duty of assisting justice.   And, after taking
counsel together, they concluded to let the matter
remain over till morning.

Imprudent determination—fatal to the end in
view!   Before the morning sun rose over the
roofs of the Nachitoches, Richard Darke, along
with several other guests of the Choctaw Chief,
had taken departure from the place.

The assassin had a second time escaped.

END OF VOL. I.

PILLING, PRINTER, GUILDFORD, SURREY.

www.ingramcontent.com/pod-product-compliance
Lightning Source LLC
Chambersburg PA
CBHW020854020726
47497CB00005B/1410